"You had to give up a lot for Mark, didn't you?"

She drew a long faltering breath. She might not quite understand Rick's game, but she refused to be beaten at it. "I didn't mind, really," she said, but her tone and expression betrayed her.

"No need to get defensive! This is pure sacrifice we're talking about—no cause for shame, surely?" He was homing in again, right on target. "Vanessa, you *did* mind! You minded a lot, didn't you? And you've never stopped minding, have you?"

"There are other things more important in life than doing what you want." It was a pious retort, and a futile one. "Anyway, once Mark's through school, once he's decided what he wants to do—well, then I'll be free to pick up where I left off."

Rick's body was tantalisingly close to hers, though scarcely touching. "Will you, Vanessa? Are you sure?"

Rowan Kirby, happily married for eighteen years to an ex-research scientist, has two teenage children and lives near Bristol. With a degree in English, she has spent time teaching English to foreign students and has been involved in adult literacy. She always wanted to write, and has had articles published in newspapers and in women's magazines.

Books by Rowan Kirby

HARLEQUIN ROMANCE
2675—SILENT STREAM
2758—HUNGER
2776—POWER POINT
2829—CONTRASTS
2847—FUSION
2873—SHADOW FALL

Harmonies

Rowan Kirby

Harlequin Books

TORONTO • NEW YORK • LONDON
AMSTERDAM • PARIS • SYDNEY • HAMBURG
STOCKHOLM • ATHENS • TOKYO • MILAN

Original hardcover edition published in 1987
by Mills & Boon Limited

ISBN 0-373-02907-1

Harlequin Romance first edition May 1988

CHAPTER ONE

VANESSA was surrounded by food. Every kitchen surface was submerged under an avalanche of fresh bread rolls—baskets of soft white, trays of chunky wholemeal. Long ones, round ones, twisted and plaited ones; granary, rye; caraway, poppy or sesame-seeded...

At the centre, where she had carefully cleared a space, were the bowls and plates overflowing with tasty fillings. Cheeses, patés, smoked salmon, olives, anchovies, crisp salads...

Vanessa was preparing a smorgasbord for the Fotherington-Smolletts' party—or rather, according to the fancy invitation cards, their At Home. It was one of her specialities, and she ought to be able to put one together standing on her head by now. But this was for thirty guests, and thirty people could engulf a whole lot of open sandwiches.

If only Kerry or Carol were here to help! Kerry might cluck, fizz and flap, but she worked like greased lightning, and four hands were so much more efficient than two, even when the two were as deft and confident as Vanessa's. As for the dependable, placid Carol, she was stuck at home today with a poorly child, not in a position to do creative things with savouries. So Vanessa was coping alone.

Still, Kerry would be here any minute now with the van, ready to help pack the goodies up and whisk them off to the ugly neo-Georgian mansion occupied by the Fotherington-Smolletts, on its imposing site overlooking the village. Then at last Vanessa could wash her hands of the day's work—not to mention the residue of butter, cream cheese, oil, wine vinegar—and sink into her favourite armchair. Perhaps enjoy a well earned sherry with some soothing music.

The last scalloped half-tomato, the final neat slice of hard-boiled egg. Reaching for the clingfilm, Vanessa glanced at the kitchen clock—and frowned. This lot was due at its destination in twenty minutes. For once Kerry, generally so punctual, was late. But Vanessa never admitted panic. Keeping calm, in charge, on top of events: that was another of her specialities. Even more of an expertise than smorgasbord—or for that matter *coq au vin*, lasagne or Waldorf salad.

Main courses and savouries were her forté. She left most of the sweets to Carol, who excelled at those gooey, creamy concoctions with which clients expected to entertain their guests. Kerry supervised the equipment and transport. The three of them made an excellent team. Trade had boomed, spreading to neighbouring villages and local towns along with their reputation.

Now the telephone trilled impatiently from the wall opposite. Vanessa sighed as she transferred most of the stickiness from her fingers on to a clean, damp towel—always handily placed for the purpose—then ruined the effect by wiping them dry on her jeans as she answered the summons.

'Doorsteps. How can we help you?' The standard official greeting emerged more spontaneously now than her own name. As if her personality had been swallowed up into the business—her own real pres-

sures safely wrapped in its safer, more manageable
ones.

'Vanessa? It's me!'

'Carol? What's going on? It's nearly five! Kerry
should be round here and loading by this time. I'm
just . . .'

'That's the point, she can't! That's why I'm
phoning.'

'What do you mean, can't?' No panic—never
that—but an edge of anxiety, just creeping in to
harden Vanessa's level, gentle, musical tone.

'She's just been on the phone to me, in a state.
The van's broken down. Apparently she's tried
everything she can think of, and nothing's doing:
Gertrude's gone dead on us.'

'Blast!' This had to be serious. If anyone could
get action out of the internal combustion engine,
it was Kerry. She understood Gertrude's myste-
rious workings as a surgeon knows the human body.
'But why did she phone *you*? Why not get straight
on to *me*?'

'She was due here first, to collect the gateaux,
remember? One Black Forest, two strawberry
cheesecakes—I've got them all ready. I said I'd
warn you, while she had another wrestle with the
cranking handle, just in case.'

'OK, no problem. I can easily load this lot into
the car. After all, that was why I chose the
hatchback in the first place. Thank goodness there's
nothing hot in the order.' Vanessa's mind was
surging ahead. 'I'll be with you in about ten
minutes, all right? Meanwhile, can you get back to
Kerry and tell her not to rupture herself, it's all in
hand?'

'Of course. I'll suggest she call Mike from the garage. Last time this happened, he had Gert fixed up in no time. See you, Vanessa.'

But the line was already purring. Vanessa was on the other side of the kitchen, heading for her stack of foil containers.

Carol was waiting patiently at the door of her modern estate house on the village outskirts, clutching three large boxes. Vanessa might be in a slightly fraught state, but she registered at once that her old friend had been crying.

'Hey, what is it? Has something happened? Is Johnny worse?'

Carol shook her head. 'A bit feverish still. Subdued, that's all—he'll be fine in a couple of days. Just that we have to be careful with his chest, you know, after that last attack of...'

'So what's the matter?' Vanessa took the boxes, but stayed where she was. Some things in life were more important than a few greedy diners, and she was very fond of Carol.

'Nothing, honestly. Well, something very silly. I won't tell you now or you'll get even later. I'll phone this evening, if that's all right.'

'Of course it's all right! If you're sure. Perhaps I'd better not stop...'

'No, they'll be drooling for their dinner.' Carol achieved an unconvincing smile.

Vanessa still hesitated. 'Give me a ring, then. Promise?'

'I will.' Carol drew a deep breath as Vanessa turned away. 'Actually, Vanessa...talking of rings...there might be one small favour you could do for me, after you've been up to Highview—it's on your way back—if you have a few moments...'

Vanessa swung round instantly, in response to the sharp note of appeal. 'Tell me.'

'I've...you see, I've gone and lost my wedding ring. It's a bit loose and it must have slipped off. Ken and I had a bit of a row last night, then this morning I discovered...'

'Another row?' Vanessa put the boxes down on the step. Her dark eyes were warm with concern. 'Oh, Carol, I'm sorry to hear this!'

Carol shrugged. 'As I say, I found my wedding ring missing, and somehow—I know it sounds silly, but it seemed to make the whole thing much worse, as if...' Tears glistened in her eyes again.

'I can understand, I really can. It doesn't sound at all silly. Sort of symbolic?'

'That's just it. And I don't dare tell Ken. He's being so unpredictable at the moment, Vanessa. He snaps at me, and that upsets Johnny, and starts me off again. I know I'm too sensitive, but I do hate being shouted at.'

'Of course you do—of course!' Vanessa's hand reached out to touch Carol's arm. 'You're not too sensitive, you're just human. Look, it's bound to turn up—your ring, I mean. I'll come and help you look for it, if you like, as soon as I've delivered this lot safe and...'

'No, that's what I was trying to say. The thing is, yesterday evening, before Johnny got worse, I was round at the church. It's my turn to tidy up and do the flowers this week, and I spent about half an hour there, pottering about, you know...I think I must have dropped it while I was there. I've scoured the house, and I'm sure it's not here. I was carrying vases around, and filling them from that sink in the vestry, and I thought maybe...'

'You'd like me to go and have a look? Say no more! Just let me organise these Fotherington-Whatsits, and I'll be up at the church, have a thorough look. Leave no hassock unturned.'

'Would you really?'

Vanessa was brisk and positive, in direct response to the dawning hope in Carol's face. 'Try stopping me! But now I really must get this stuff delivered, or we'll have a riot on our hands. See you later—and *don't worry*!'

Vanessa stooped to pick up the cake boxes, then turned and marched down the path, waving her free hand once as she went.

Johnny was complaining, but Carol stayed to watch her friend go. Vanessa was five years her junior—and single. But life had been tough on her, bringing the kind of maturity which deepens with suffering. A wealth of perception that would have been uncommon in a person twice her age. It was only a pity this clear-eyed sympathy didn't extend inwards, into herself. In her contacts with other people—their needs, their feelings—she was exceptionally aware. Where her own emotions and desires were concerned, her humanity lurked behind a block as solid as a skyscraper.

Carol supposed it was hardly surprising, considering the challenges Vanessa had faced in twenty-three short years. The adult sacrifices she'd made; the profound decisions she'd been pressed to take. Sad, but not surprising.

Ah, well, they all had their problems. They rallied round one another. That's what friends and colleagues were for.

Colleagues... Carol was smiling faintly as she turned back to the house, where her small son was becoming more hoarsely imperious by the minute. Yes, they all had their responsibilities. The business was one of them, of course, though it often seemed a relief, a holiday from the more intense hassles of domestic life.

Doorsteps—born from a brainwave of Vanessa's, three years ago now. The idea had been to set up a simple little service, making and delivering simple little snacks and sandwiches. But it had blossomed, through her flair and determination, complemented by the respective qualities of Kerry and Carol. They all had reason to be proud: it was a success story of our time. Not only were they gaining dignity and satisfaction, they were even making some money, which couldn't be bad.

The one cloud on Carol's horizon was this uncomfortable, inexplicable burst of irascibility from her husband, Ken. Always such an even, good-natured man, up until recently. Quiet, unassuming, kind... but now, suddenly, he had turned difficult. Carol muttered a private prayer under her breath, as she went to comfort her fretful child.

St Saviour's kept its ancient watch over the village, peaceful in this early spring twilight: still and stately, its square stone tower so permanent against a deepening violet sky.

The churchyard was shadowed, but not at all sinister. Vanessa was no regular attender, but she liked to know it was there. It had always seemed to her that there was so much more of life than of death in this place, especially just now, with new daffodils and crocuses, the last of the snowdrops, and that tender green of young leaves and grass.

The stained glass windows were illuminated; the heavy oak door moved at her touch. Someone was here, no doubt about that. Their presence was strong—alarmingly potent, a total experience which swamped Vanessa as she crossed the threshold, through the curved arch, into the nave.

Abruptly she stopped and stood motionless, staring about her, every sense tingling. Gradually, this strange engulfing of her whole self ebbed away as her rational mind took charge. How ludicrous! Next thing, she'd be having mystic or religious visions! Vanessa Davies of all people: she of the hard head, the sharp wit—acknowledged servant and mistress of the great god Reason.

Certainly most of her senses were involved in this enveloping aura. The sight of muted colours and sweeping Gothic lines; the smell of old musty books and new polish; the feel of cold flagstones through thin canvas shoes, along with a prickle of evening chill on her skin. But above all, sound.

Music, of course. Classical music: her grand passion. Sometimes she pushed it to the side of her life, for private reasons; but always it fought back, enfolding her, becoming inevitable and inescapable when no other level of existence seemed high enough.

It could have been so much more than a source of comfort and pleasure in her life—if things had been different. It should have been her destiny, the core of her present and her future, her whole preoccupation, if only...if only...

But fate had intervened. Tragic necessity had shaped her choices. Vanessa was not given to pointless regrets or empty pining. Music would always be there, whether or not she decided to spend her own days in creating it. She couldn't afford—in any sense of the word—to risk indulging herself now, actively training, studying to spin that magic to end all magics. For the moment she must stay here, in the family home, with Mark. Where she belonged.

Her chosen role was that of listener, passive audience. She must never let herself forget that, whatever urges tempted her in other directions.

And she listened now, as this cascade of notes flowed from the mellowed organ pipes. Fierce, even violent, raging and billowing to every corner of the church. Their impact was physical—a devastating assault on her ears and emotions which had knocked her off balance. Recovering, she paused to evaluate what she was actually hearing.

As far as she was aware, the usual organist's repertoire consisted largely of *Sheep May Safely Graze*, the *Wedding March* and a popular assortment of anthems and hymn tunes. This, unless Vanessa was much mistaken, was an extremely advanced and complicated piece, highly unlikely to be numbered among Mrs Fennell's accomplishments. Offhand, Vanessa could think of few people in the village who might recognise it, let alone play it.

Natural reserve was overwhelmed by acute curiosity. Vanessa was drawn, magnetised to the source of these sounds. Presumably they must emanate from human hands—but for a few fanciful seconds, even she could imagine some spiritual agent at

work. Or perhaps the fine old instrument was
playing itself?

The organist's niche was an enclosed space, snug
behind the controls like a pilot in a cockpit. In order
to keep tabs on what the vicar and congregation
were up to, Mrs Fennell insisted on having a mirror
attached to the front of her little bothy—on exactly
the same principle, she frequently explained, as the
rear-view mirror in a car. Approaching the organ
loft from behind and at an angle, Vanessa could
see nothing of the organist at all—and then, suddenly, a pair of eyes gazed straight back at her, reflected in this mirror.

They were a startlingly vivid blue: wide-set, wide
open, faintly humorous—and fixed firmly on her
face.

Too late to retreat, so she boldly moved closer.
Now, from one side, she registered the frame that
went with the eyes. Young. Male. Sitting up tall,
clad informally in denims and shirtsleeves.
Shoulders and arms at once rangy but powerful,
directing long, sure fingers across those twin keyboards. Fast, delicate; strong, confident. Picking
out chords, melodies, harmonies as if by instinct
from the stratosphere.

Thick blond hair, close-cropped to a well shaped
head. Fair brows, slanting, quizzical. Profile clean
and rather sharp, with that long nose and jutting
chin. Small ears; chiselled, expressive lips.

All this Vanessa noticed subliminally, at an inner
level. More consciously, she only knew that he
played like an angel, and continued playing, never
faltering—as if her arrival was simply part of the
atmosphere he conjured up. As if he had expected
her; created her deliberately, along with the music.

She also knew that the blue eyes were intent on her, roving across her form and features as tangibly as his hands communicated with the keys.

What they saw was a sweet oval face, a slight, rounded figure in jeans and a bottle-green sweater with white woolly sheep grazing all over it. Hair the colour of high-quality bitter chocolate, long and rippling, pulled into a loose pony-tail to hang down her back; a deep fringe sweeping arched dark brows; enigmatic brown eyes. An expression which combined gravity with optimism. A bruised acceptance of the world—positive, yet withdrawn, philosophical, yet wounded.

The interest deepened in his own eyes, but he went on playing. Then, quite suddenly, he stopped. His hands remained on the keys, but the sound died away—slowly, as the air left the pipes, an eerie, disconcerting whine. He was not smiling, but somehow Vanessa had the impression that he was.

The silence was even louder than the music, and far less enjoyable. It seemed endless; but eventually he swivelled on the stool to face her directly, still regarding her with that candid appraisal.

'That's better. I don't mind an audience, but I do prefer to be able to see them properly. See what I'm up against.'

His voice was not particularly deep, but very resonant—considered, utterly assured, like his playing. The accent was vaguely south-eastern. Most probably a metropolitan, a Londoner, not a local like Vanessa. One thing was certain: she had never seen him before. At least, she was pretty sure she hadn't. On the other hand, there was something— a hint of recognition . . . a suggestion . . .

'I don't care to be at a disadvantage.' He was still talking, and looking, and she was rudely staring. 'I don't like being stalked.'

Vanessa rarely blushed, but she did it now. 'I'm— I'm sorry. It was just that we don't often—I don't often hear anyone playing like that.'

'So brilliantly, you mean?'

It might be arrogant, but it was accurate. 'Not in here, no.' Then enthusiasm overcame her disapproval. 'It sounded wonderful. And you aren't even using any *music*! It was César Franck, wasn't it?'

The eyes narrowed, flippant yet serious. 'That's right. One of the all-time greats, *Prelude, Chorale and Fugue*.'

'I know! One of my favourites, too!' Vanessa was quite breathless. 'I used to be able to struggle through the first couple of pages on the piano, but could never get any further than that. I've never even dared *try* that part you were playing. I mean, you only have to look at it on the page! I couldn't even begin to decipher it!'

It was against her nature, expressing such open admiration. But where was the point in hypocrisy, on this of all subjects? She was enthralled.

'So you're a pianist, then?' His arms were folded across his chest now, hands tucked in as if to prevent them straying back to those enticing keys and stops.

'No, no. I just play around. I had lessons as a child, but I'm not really...my real...' She swallowed, looking away. 'I wasn't much good at it,' she announced firmly. 'I just love music, that's all.'

If he heard the tightness in her voice, saw the veil fall over her eyes, he refrained from comment.

He merely nodded and gestured to the keys with one hand.

'Never had a go at this lot, then?'

'Good heavens, no! I'm not nearly good enough for that. I'd make a terrible hash of it. I don't even know how it works.'

'Nothing to it, really. I'll show you, if you like.'

'No, I . . . well, I . . . I mustn't stop. Thanks all the same. Are you—have you come from far? Are you visiting? Staying in the village?'

She was gabbling, and she knew it, but for obscure reasons all her defences had suddenly sprung into action.

'In a manner of speaking, yes. Staying in the village, that's right. Recharging the batteries, and partaking of a bit of country air.'

It was Vanessa's turn to nod, without surprise. People came and stayed here all the time, in this picturesque heart of south-west England. Holidays, retreats, welcome breaks from city life. Residents took it in their stride; in fact, a good many of them drew a living from it.

'The vicar kindly let me have a loan of his keyboards.' It was a strange way of putting it, but Vanessa let that pass. 'Thursday's a good day, he told me—early evening—so here I am. No one would disturb me,' he added pointedly, 'if I came then. No campanologists. No oratorios. No evening benedictions. No christenings, funerals or weddings. Just me and this wonderful lady here.'

Vanessa's head jerked up sharply, but his expression was solemn, and he was still indicating the organ keys as he spoke. She relaxed into a smile. 'How do you know it's female?'

'What else could she be? All that wind and commotion, channelled into such sweet music when you know how to handle her?'

If he expected outrage, he was going to be disappointed. Vanessa's smile broadened. If there was a twinge of irritation, it was far outweighed by a new, unexpected frisson of excitement at the image.

'Are most instruments female, then?'

He thought about it, absent-mindedly drumming those long fingers on the silent keys. 'In a way, I suppose you could say so. As I just said, you have to know your way around them to get results. And when you do——' he whistled softly, espressively, '—nothing like it!'

Vanessa decided the analogy had gone far enough. What was she doing, actively encouraging such double-talk, and with a stranger? However gifted; however fascinating.

'Well, I'm sorry I disturbed your peace. I wouldn't normally be here. Not on a Thursday evening, or any other time, come to that. I came to look for something. A friend lost a ring, and she thinks she might have dropped it here, so I said I'd come and see, because she can't get away...'

She trailed off, staring past him, awkward. Why tell him all this? He just wanted to get on with his playing, and quite right too.

But he showed no sign of impatience or annoyance. 'A truly selfless act of Christian charity. Very suitable in this setting.'

Was he mocking? Or not? Vanessa, usually an excellent judge of character, found herself floundering in the face of this one. 'Yes, so if you'll excuse me, I'll get on and search. But don't mind me, I mean, please do go on playing while I...'

Please do go on playing, she echoed to herself.
I could listen to you all night.

'Perhaps I could help?' He half rose, with a
natural chivalry, sharply set off against the slight
edge of satire. Long legs unravelled themselves from
beneath the stool. His jeans were straight and tight.
He wore somewhat dilapidated trainers, in well
scuffed leather.

His hips were very slim in the clinging denim.
Vanessa's hands thrust themselves into the pockets
of her own jeans—an old, spontaneous, ineffectual
gesture of self-protection.

'No, no, that's OK, I'd far rather listen to you
play!' She kept her eyes on his face—which seemed,
at this moment, the least threatening part of him.
'Anyway...' she collected herself, and her voice
dropped a full three tones, 'you've been disrupted
more than enough already.'

'Disrupted, huh? Is that what I've been?'

He had these lucid ocean eyes, and they were
definitely glinting.

'You know what I mean...'

'Yes, I'll go along with you on that.' He was
sitting again now, sideways on the stool, legs
stretched out so that they reached almost to where
she stood; so that his feet, in the shabby trainers,
came within half an inch of hers, in their neat blue
canvas boots. 'I'd say it wasn't a bad sort of word
for what I've been. Disrupted.'

He nodded, meditatively, and the eyes never left
her face. Still defensive, Vanessa frowned, biting
her lip.

Then she smiled. It was not a conscious act of
provocation or defiance—quite the reverse; but

perhaps one layer of her feminine soul was well aware of the effect it would have.

'I'll leave you to it, then. Don't mind me if I grovel about a bit. My friend thinks she might have dropped this ring when she was arranging flowers, so I might have to...'

'That's a relief,' he interrupted.

Vanessa was disconcerted all over again. 'How do you mean?'

'From what you said before, I imagined this wedding fiasco, where the best man drops the ring at the crucial moment. Or the groom fumbles while placing aforementioned ring on the bride's finger. Or the bride seizes it and throws it in the groom's face, screaming that she prefers another.'

Vanessa chuckled. 'Nothing like that. We don't go in for such melodrama in Compton Magna,' she remarked. 'We're a staid and steady community.' On the surface of it, at least. Underneath...

'Rubbish.' Her thoughts might have been a video display unit. 'No community's that staid, not when you penetrate beneath the serene exterior. City, country, I happen to think it's the same wherever you go. The pace might be faster or slower, but basically, all human life is there.'

After a brief pause, during which Vanessa studied her feet and he studied her face, she raised her eyes and said sweetly, 'I expect you're right. But I don't suppose you'll be with us long enough to find out. I hope you enjoy your stay, anyway. And the rest of your session on our lovely old organ. We're proud of it, you know. It's good to hear it being properly treated for a change.'

'I'll do my best.' He swivelled round again to face the keys. His hands and feet were already searching, finding their way back into the music; picking up where they had left off. 'Just let me get the bellows going again...here we are...right.' He turned to her, but she thought his attention was more than half-way elsewhere. Such intense concentration—so easily broken, yet so swiftly restored! How she envied it! 'Hope you find the ring,' he called, as she turned to go.

'Thanks.' She flashed him a smile over her shoulder.

He watched her, in his mirror, until she had disappeared round the corner, out of sight. Then he began to play. Restrained at first, then rising to a full, frenzied crescendo.

This time, the swelling cadences of a Bach toccata. Vanessa's heart lifted and filled out like the sails of a yacht in a summer wind.

Under the influence of that genius—or whatever spell was at work—she headed straight into the vestry, straight over to the sink in the corner. She picked up the soap and looked in the dish beneath it. For several seconds, she stared at the plain gold band which lurked there among the slime and suds.

Carol's ring; just like that! She hadn't even had to look, or bend, still less grovel. Intuition had pointed her unerringly to it, against the accompanying grandeur of Bach. Marvellous! Elating!

She almost skipped to the door of the church. Before opening it she hesitated, swung round and gazed over towards the organ loft. The sound seemed to penetrate every cell of her, as if she saw it and felt it as well as heard it. All her nerve-endings were alerted, alive to it.

Her mind's eye pictured the fingers which were now in the magic process of producing it. Fine-boned, firm hands, wrists, arms: lightly tanned, blond-haired...

Her own fingers closed tight on Carol's ring. Top priority now was to return it to an anxious Carol, before Ken missed it.

She shoved the precious object into her purse, safe among far less important pounds and pence. Then, with a last glance round the church, a last lingering moment to relish the music, she shut the door quietly behind her.

A minute later she was in her car, roaring off down the road and through the sleepy village.

CHAPTER TWO

NUMBER three, East Street had been Vanessa's home for as long as she could remember. The family had moved there from industrial South Wales when she had been no more than a toddler. Centre of a row of Victorian cottages, a sloping, uneven terrace, just off-centre of a traditional English village. Not too far from bustling towns, a major city, motorways, railways—yet tucked into folds of verdant landscape. Surely, Vanessa often told herself, the ideal way to live? The ideal place, the ideal pace?

So why did she find it so hard to believe herself? Why did she secretly hanker for brighter lights, some kind of sophistication? Why this niggling resentment—never articulated, always suppressed—that fate had deprived her of a whole section of carefree, socialising youth? There was nothing to be done about it, even if it had.

Now she sank into an armchair in the long, open-plan living-room—sitting area at one end, kitchen at the other—with a sherry at her elbow and a record on the turntable. Her stereo system was one of her few indulgences. More vital than clothes or furniture. More necessary than food and drink. Without good music there would be no value in living at all.

The Mozart Clarinet Quintet reached out its glorious tendrils to fill the room, the house. Vanessa closed her eyes and breathed it in, letting it become her world. Such spectacular arpeggios, rising to peaks; such rare quality of tone! The clarinet seemed to her the nearest artificial equivalent to the human voice, especially sympathetic when it was interpreting such smooth, profound, lyrical, *healing* melodies as Mozart's . . .

The front door slammed. Her eyes screwed themselves up tight, and her fists clenched. Tonight's allocation of peace had been short-lived. Not even enough to get to the end of the first movement.

She waited for the inevitable series of thumps and crashes which can only be produced by a teenage boy in his normal progress through life. Each wall, floor, piece of furniture becomes instantly noisier, more fragile, the moment they touch it.

Vanessa had decided this must be a strict natural law. Mark had never been a particularly clumsy child, but he had expanded into this gangling creature, somewhere between boy and man but uncomfortable with both—a full head taller than herself, but still all bones, angles and feet. One minute, she had been looking down at the top of his head, and that trusting little hand would reach up to hold hers; then they had been on a level, sharing laughter and sorrow on an equal physical basis; now she had to stare upwards into his face. Into those dark, expressive eyes, reminiscent of her own. Confusing for her, and no doubt for him.

Tonight the sound effects were doubled and punctuated with raucous chortles and conversation. So, her brother had a friend with him. Or probably two—that was more than likely. A gregarious species, Vanessa had also discovered, the adolescent youth; liking to travel in packs.

She stayed put, but heaved a deep sigh, knowing what was about to happen. They clumped upstairs to Mark's room, directly above this one. Within a minute, the relentless throb of a rock group effortlessly penetrated the carpet, floorboards, ceiling, and Vanessa's head. Mozart's delicate phrases were utterly eclipsed.

She never failed to be furious—and amazed. It was like a drug. They had to switch it on the instant they arrived, as if they couldn't even breathe without it. Pathetic! And all of it the same strident, unsubtle racket! At least when she had been their age, the pop scene had included some reasonably pleasant songs—simple ballads, a few decent tunes and harmonies. Things she could just about identify with, even though she had much preferred the true classics from the moment she could make a distinction. But now the whole business seemed to have deteriorated, sunk to a crass, coarse level, so that Vanessa could no longer tolerate or fathom it.

But she had to share the house with Mark. And he tended to point out, with infuriating logic, that she had set up *her* musical tastes in their mutual living-room, so why shouldn't he enjoy *his* in his own bedroom? Which might have been fair comment, except that when it came to a straight contest, his kind of music—if you could grace it with the label—won hands down every time, through sheer volume.

The first side of the Mozart ended, but Vanessa didn't bother to get up and turn it over. If anything, the clash of the two was worse than Mark's dreadful din on its own. In a few minutes, when she'd finished her sherry, she'd go and say hello, ask them to turn it down a bit, see if they wanted a cup of tea, but just now she felt too tired and too comfortable to move from her chair.

Ten seconds later, the noise stopped as abruptly as it had started. Further bumps and thuds indicated that they were on their way downstairs. Then they were in the kitchen, foraging for nourishment.

It was dark now, but she had deliberately left the lights off, appreciating the restful effect of dusk through undrawn curtains. No doubt Mark assumed she was either still out, or in her room with her feet up. She really was very weary, and they could manage perfectly well without her. She leaned back again, sipping her sherry.

She knew Mark's companion as soon as he spoke. Stewart, his best friend in the village, a likeable boy, shorter and stockier than Mark, with a thatch of sandy hair. His parents ran the local post office.

'Tea?' Mark was filling the kettle. 'Coffee, or what?'

'Hey, what's all this stuff?' Stewart's muffled tones came from the larder. 'Sandwiches or something?'

'Let's see...oh, that'll be smorgasbord,' Mark told him airily.

'Smorgaswhat?'

'Sort of posh Swedish snacks. She often makes it for clients. If she's left all that out, it means we can eat it. It's lush, especially that pink stuff. That's smoked salmon.'

''I *know*. What d'you think I am, a wally? D'you think I've never seen smoked salmon?' Stewart complained, through a hefty mouthful of Vanessa's efforts. 'Hey, Mark, have you heard this one? What did the elephant say to the naked man?'

Mark groaned. 'Everyone's heard that one, a million years ago. Where do you get your jokes, out of the *Beano*? Pass that jar over there, will you? The one that says Tea. And that other one, that says Sugar?'

Stewart, still chewing energetically, tried another topic for entertainment. 'Did you hear what happened to Shirley Price, at that party we never went to? Her contact lens fell into her drink!'

'Oh, yeah? Did she get it back?'

'No way.' Stewart spluttered with glee. Vanessa was only too glad she couldn't actually see what was happening to her cherished salmon rolls—rejects or not. 'That's the best part. She didn't realize it had fallen out till it was too late and then she'd finished her drink.' He was half speechless with mirth. 'Can you *believe* it? *Drank* her contact lens!'

''If she'd drunk it, how did she know it was there in the first place?' Mark had a sharper turn of mind, and a less credulous one.

'Oh, I don't know. It had fallen out before. It often does when she gets a bit... you know. That's what Sharron told me, anyway, and she was *there*.'

'That's nothing. I heard a much better one from Clive, you know, that bloke in the Lower Sixth, did the lighting for our last Drama production. Here, have some tea. Get the milk out of the fridge.'

'What was that, then?'

'His old man went to this party, and drank too much. New Year's Eve, it was. Got really sloshed, sick as a dog, then went to the bathroom. Then felt better and went back to the party.'

'So what?' Stewart slurped tea, so loudly that Vanessa could hear it from the other end of the room.

'I haven't got to the point yet. So his wife says, where's your teeth? He says, how do you mean, where's my teeth? In my mouth, of course. And she says, your false teeth, they aren't in. You know what he'd gone and done? Here, have one of these, they're that holey cheese, you know, what's it called? Emmental. Great.'

'He'd taken his dentures out when he was sick?' Stewart hazarded.

'Much worse. He was too drunk to remember, so they fell out, didn't they? He never realised, so naturally he flushed them away, never to be seen again.' Mark was a born performer. Even Vanessa had to smile at this gruesomely unpleasant tale.

'Oh, my God! Flushed his teeth down the loo! Oh, wow! *Bad* one!' Stewart fell about, a grateful public.

Vanessa decided it was time to make her presence known. She was enjoying this exchange a lot better than their so-called music, but if the level of conversation sank much lower, it could prove embarrassing for all concerned.

She yawned loudly, stretched, then reached out to switch on the table lamp beside her. There was a significant pause from the kitchen regions, followed by Mark's voice. 'Hi! Ness, is that you?'

'I hope so. Who else were you expecting?'

'Sorry, never realised you were down here. Why didn't you say something? Were you asleep?'

'Resting, that's all. I've had a busy day. How was yours?'

'OK. Want a cup of tea?'

'Wouldn't mind. I'll come in, shall I?'

'No, I'll bring it over there. Want one of your rolls?'

'Yes please. A paté one, if you've left any.'

'They're really great, Vanessa.' Recovering from the acute shock of finding Mark's elder sister eavesdropping on his every word, Stewart switched on his best manners. 'Delicious.'

'Stewart's here,' Mark explained unnecessarily.

'So I gathered. Hello, Stewart. How was the rehearsal?'

'It went quite well.' Stewart was all charm, intent on making up for his uncouth assault on her sandwiches. 'Are you coming to see the play?'

'Of course. Part of your Drama Practical, isn't it?'

'That's right. We have to perform it, before the actual O-levels.'

Mark came into the sitting-room, bearing a mug of tea and a plate. 'Talking of O-levels, I've got something to ask you, Ness.'

'Oh yes? Thanks.' She took the plate and mug. 'Why don't you sit down? Come in and join us, Stewart. Bring some more rolls with you. They won't keep—might as well finish them off.'

Stewart sidled in, looking sheepish. 'I've had enough, thanks, Vanessa. I expect they'll have supper waiting for me at home. But they were really nice,' he assured her.

'They should be. The punters pay enough for them,' Mark commented.

'I'll have you know, little brother, those punters help keep you in guitar strings and cassettes!'

Mark was ready for that one. This ground had been trodden before. 'No, they don't! I buy all my own music stuff, out of my earnings at the shop, and you know it!'

'Yes, yes, and you get them at a hefty discount. Cushiest thing you ever landed, that Saturday job.'

'Nothing cushy about it! Judgement, intelligence, entrepreneurial instinct, that's what it takes.'

It was impossible to be irritated with Mark for long. Vanessa lapsed into affectionate amusement, as she usually did. 'OK, so you buy all that for yourself. Quite right too. I should have said, they keep you in baked beans and toothbrushes.'

'Who needs baked beans and toothbrushes?'

'Who needs your kind of music?' Vanessa countered.

This banter was a kind of game—a real form of communication common to all brothers and sisters, but even more important to Vanessa and Mark. They had done it since Mark was very small, but now they were thrown together, more interdependent than the younger generation of any other family might expect to be; and this only resulted in more of it.

'Who needs *your* kind?' Mark was retorting, instantly.

Stewart looked at his watch and cleared his throat. 'Think I'd better be going. Mum'll be wondering...'

'Hang on a minute, Stew.' Mark grabbed his friend's arm to prevent him sloping off. 'I wanted you to be here, when I tell Ness about—you know.'

'Oh, yeah.' Stewart sat down again, but on the edge of his chair.

'About what?' Vanessa finished her tea and put the cup down.

'Well——' Mark drew a deep breath. Vanessa immediately became guarded. She knew this expression of old. It was the one that said, you're not going to think much of this, but I intend to have my own way, anyway. 'You remember they wanted us to do some work experience this half-term, but I couldn't think of anything to do, so I didn't?'

'We couldn't agree on anything suitable,' Vanessa corrected primly. She turned to Stewart. 'What did *you* do? Anything interesting?'

'My father got me into this bank for three days.'

Vanessa smiled. 'No need to sound so gloomy about it.'

'He feels gloomy about it,' Mark said. 'So would I. Who wants to work in a bank?'

'Lots of people would be only too pleased to work in a bank.'

'Oh, Vanessa, you're so—uncool! I mean, it's bad enough when people's *parents* are like that, but you're hardly any older than *we* are, for God's sake!'

Mark's explosions were rare, but when they came, they were aimed below the belt, and generally more through desperation than cruelty. But Vanessa had hardened herself against all this. Her sacrifices had not been—would not be—in vain. You couldn't expect sunshine and gratitude from a gawky adolescent, especially a male. In time, Mark would appreciate what she had done for him, the directions she had pushed him in, and why.

After a short, tense silence, she coughed and said, 'So, what's this thing you wanted to tell me? Something to do with the work experience? Have you had another idea, because if so I hope it's more . . .'

'That's just it. You see, I was talking to Mr Scully—the new music teacher at school, started this term, you know—and——'

'He's nothing like old Braithwaite,' Stewart put in, helpfully. 'Really young and trendy. Wears drainpipes, listens to Status Quo, likes Billy Bragg and everything.'

Mark glared at Stewart. This was support he could do without. 'Bit of an ageing juvenile, as a matter of fact. Anyway, I was talking to him, and he said, guess who's coming to the area? To your own village, to be precise? The actual manor house at Compton Magna?'

'That huge place up Beacon Hill? But it's been empty for...'

'Well, it's not going to be empty any more. Because guess who's coming to live in it?' He was all excited now, flushed and eager. Vanessa grew more suspicious than ever.

'How the hell am I supposed to know? Samantha Fox? Joan Collins?'

Stewart giggled, but Mark ignored his sister's heavy irony. 'Try again. A really big name: even you'll have heard of this one.'

Vanessa shrugged. 'Ian Botham? Basil Brush?'

Mark leaned forwards, with the air of a man about to divulge a top state secret. 'Only Rick Seymour, that's all.'

'Rick Seymour.' Vanessa looked blank. 'Should it mean something to me? Because I'm sorry to say it doesn't.'

Stewart's mouth dropped open, and Mark tutted in exasperation. 'Vanessa, it really is too much. *Too much*! I mean, *everyone* knows who he is. I mean, you don't even have to like pop music to know...'

Vanessa turned to Stewart, appealing. No use expecting any sense out of the seething Mark. 'Who,' she enquired mildly, 'is this Rick Seymour when he's at home? Or indeed, when he's at the manor house in Compton Magna? Put me out of my misery, Stewart.'

Stewart rose gallantly to the challenge. Privately, he considered Vanessa pretty amazing—really nice, and sexy with it, but of course he could never even hint as much to Mark about his sister. Especially not in their situation. It would be more like confessing that you fancied someone's *mother*!

'Totem.' He nodded significantly.

'Totem.' Vanessa stared at him, then at Mark. 'As in pole?'

'Right. It's a group. A band,' Stewart explained, as patiently as he knew how. It was hard to believe anyone, even Vanessa with her renowned hostility to that kind of music, hadn't heard of Totem. Weird.

'Up and coming, are they?' Vanessa made the effort to sound keen.

'Upped and come. They've arrived. Ness, they're *famous*! Rick Seymour is a—a really *Great Musician*.' Mark was emphasising each syllable, waving both hands. His voice had gone cracked and squeaky. 'Totem is a fantastic group. Unique. Different.'

'Brilliant,' Stewart added, for good measure.

'I'm sorry to disappoint you, but I've neither heard them, nor heard of them. Nor have I heard of Rick—what did you call him?—Seymour. Get to the point, please, Mark. So, he's coming to Compton, to the old Manor, and he plays in this band, this—Totem. So what?'

'He doesn't play *in* the band. He *is* the band. Without him, it would be just another group. He's ace. He plays everything: lead, bass, synth, drums.

He sings, and writes all their lyrics. It's good stuff, Vanessa, not the kind you don't like, you know—proper tunes and harmonies and really meaningful words and...oh, for Heaven's sake, you *must* have heard me play it!'

Mark subsided, agonised. 'It all sounds the same to me,' Vanessa remarked coldly.

Mark sighed heavily. This was a real uphill struggle, but he'd known it would be, and he needed her approval so he must persevere. 'Well, the point is, Scully says he met Rick Seymour at this gig in Bristol which he was helping to organise, and...'

'*Met* him!' Stewart sprang into life, scarlet-faced. 'You never told me this bit, Mark! Lucky b——'

'So anyway,' Mark interrupted loudly, 'he told Scully he was buying this big old place out here, and converting some of it to recording studios, setting up his company there as well as living in it, so...'

'*Recording studios!*'

Vanessa and Stewart echoed the phrase exactly in unison, but with diametrically opposite expressions. Stewart was absolutely riveted. Vanessa was aghast.

'Yes, and the thing is, Scully phoned him—after I said I hadn't found anything to fix up for work experience. And he said I could go up there, when he's settled in, watch them rehearse and record...maybe even get to play my guitar with them a bit, see what it's like with the real thing. It's the chance of a lifetime, Vanessa, you've got to realise...'

Pale with intense effort and emotion, Mark slumped. There was nothing to do now but wait

and see how she was going to take it. She wasn't
always predictable. Not always. There had to be
hope.

Vanessa was thinking hard, that much was obvious. Hands clasped in her lap, head bent, in that
attitude he knew so well: the one which meant
something extremely complex and tricky was fil-
tering through her mind. This surprised Mark, for
two reasons. First, she hadn't leaped into instant
negative dismissal of anything remotely connected
with the wonderful world of rock music. Second,
she seemed so struck—so involved—so *gripped* by
what he had just told her. Very strange.

'Vanessa?' he prompted hoarsely, at last, when
the silence stretched unbearably. Stewart was staring
at his hands and shuffling his feet.

Vanessa's head jerked up. When she did finally
speak, Mark was more surprised than ever.

'What does he look like? This—Seymour?'

'Look like?' What did this have to do with anything? Mark turned to his friend for moral support.
'What does Rick Seymour look like?'

'Oh...tallish, thinnish, fairish. Sort of good-
looking, all the women seem to think so, anyway.
I mean, Cath thinks so, and Mum thinks so, and
Shirley Price's wall is covered in pictures of him,
so...'

'Got these really blue eyes. Sometimes wears a
gold ear-ring.' Mark searched for inspiration. De-
scribing men's appearances was not part of his daily
routine. He didn't really notice such details.

'Haven't you got a poster of Totem?' Stewart
suggested. 'I'm sure you used to. Or there's the
album sleeve of *Russian Roulette*—the one with the

song about Vietnam—got him on the front, in fatigue gear, remember?'

'I did have a poster on my wall, actually, a few months back,' Mark confirmed. 'I took it down to make way for Subhumans. Or was it Half Man Half Biscuit? Anyway, I only had room for one.'

None of this was relevant to Vanessa, who seemed to have gone into a kind of peculiar trance. 'Did you say he sometimes plays other instruments? Not just guitar?'

Mark stared at her. She was speaking so slowly, deliberately, as if she was working something very difficult out as she went along. 'Percussion's one of his best things. He's really fast and versatile. And he writes all their songs, I told you. He's quite nifty on keyboards.'

Quite nifty on keyboards. Fairish. Tallish. And that face, vaguely familiar...the blue eyes, the sharp features; tight jeans, shirtsleeves. She'd seen them before, of course she had—on the wall of that perpetual shambles her brother called his room.

And more recently. This very afternoon, in the organ loft at St Saviour's, up the road! Here in the village, where he was coming to live, set up his recording studios, and generally play havoc with their ordered lives...reverberate revolting noises through the tranquil countryside...lead the young astray just before their public exams...

Quite nifty on keyboards! Vanessa threw back her shining dark head, and laughed aloud.

Mark and Stewart stared harder than ever. Mark was frowning. He had never seen her like this. His sister had so many faces. Stroppy, stubborn. Humorous, kind. Gentle, cutting. Sad, thoughtful. But this was new; this was different. It made him feel anxious, as if he didn't really know her after all.

He must break into this curious mood of hers. Any reaction would be better than this one, which was no real reaction at all.

'Can't you tell me what you think of the idea? Mr Scully's idea?' he amended hastily. Better if it sounded like an official school-type proposal, rather than his own. After all, that was what it was. That was why the whole thing had such distinct possibilities.

'Mark,' she was pointing out carefully, 'it's supposed to be work experience, not some ego trip. Do you really *want* to be a rock musician? You don't, do you? So what would be the point?'

'Who says I don't? Who says it would be an ego trip?' he snapped at her challenge, then controlled himself. 'Even if I don't make a career of it, there's no reason why I can't go and find out how they do things. I mean, at a technical level. I mean, there's a crowd of *experts*, right here in the village! I mean, no one in the *world* could be a better model to learn from than Totem! I mean, Rick *Seymour!*'

'I think I've got the message, Mark.' Vanessa was giving him one of her looks, and he subsided. He knew better than to push any harder.

'No,' she made her pronouncement at last. 'I don't think it would be a very good idea. I don't think so at all.'

Up to a few minutes ago, Mark had more than half expected this, of course, but then she had really got his hopes up. Now he exploded all over again. 'But *why?* Give me one good reason. If the school's willing to back me, and Rick Sey——'

It was her turn to erupt in a rare burst of temper. '*Will* you give over talking about Rick bloody Seymour? Just cut it out, Mark, OK? I've had it up to here. I don't want to hear another word about this character, even if he's got a guaranteed place in heaven. I think it's a terrible idea for you to miss school, so near your exams, just to go and sit at the feet of some tinpot guru...' Even if...*especially* if he's a superb virtuoso interpreter of classical music on the church organ into the bargain...doubtless on the piano too. No one who can play like that has any *right* to squander their gift on trivial garbage! It's a sin—a shame—a sacrilege!

Mark's spate of arguments poured out, inevitably, automatically. Vanessa's response was predictable, but it had been worth a try. In fact he was only just starting, if battle lines were being drawn.

'But I'd only miss about three days of school! Everyone else goes! I'd just be doing it a bit late, that's all. And my GCE work's going pretty well, everyone says so...you ask my teachers if you're worried! I could afford to take a few days, Ness. Just a few *days*...'

'No, Mark. I really don't like the idea.'

She was so strangely brusque. Of course she had strong opinions on this subject, but she was soft underneath when it came to Mark, and he wasn't above exploiting that fact. Not when something as crucial as this was at stake. It might be his whole *future*, for God's sake!

'But Ness, why? *Why?*'

I wish I could really tell you, thought Vanessa. I wish I was entirely sure myself. 'I've told you, Mark.' She was firm, calm, impervious to his pleas.

'But will you at least phone Mr Scully, or go and see him? He'll tell you ... he'll explain why it's a great idea ...'

But Vanessa was on her feet, crossing the room to draw the curtains. 'I'm starving. All I've had today is bits of smorgasbord and cups of tea and coffee. Time to get something more solid together, I think.'

'*Please*, Vanessa! Just this once. It's such an amazing chance.'

She swung to face him. Taller than her he might be, but she still held the authority in this house. Arms akimbo, she rallied every ounce of it now. 'I refuse to discuss it any more, Mark. You've got eight O-levels to concentrate on. Even if you were good enough to make a career in rock music, or any music, which I doubt ...'

'You don't know good rock music when you hear it,' Mark muttered darkly.

'I just don't like the idea of you taking time off to do it now. That's all,' she lied. 'Now, who wants a plate of scrambled eggs? And I think we've got some rather good bacon.'

She was on her way to the kitchen, collecting dirty mugs and plates as she went. Mark loped behind her—sulky, but biding his time. Stewart hovered, fascinated by the whole scene. He ought to be getting home, but he was reluctant to leave such an absorbing confrontation.

It must be so weird, being brought up by a sister so much nearer your own age, and yet so much older, six years, or was it seven? In some ways Vanessa behaved just like his parents, if not more so. In others, she was more like one of his friends, which must be really difficult for Mark.

'Scrambled eggs, Stewart?' she was calling brightly from the larder.

'Er—no really, thanks. I should've been home ages ago.'

'Want a lift?'

'Oh, no, I've got my bike.'

Vanessa was beating a bowl of eggs with a whisk. The look in her eye was determined, with an unnatural brightness. 'Some time, Mark, would you show me that poster? Of—Totem?' Her colour was high, but Stewart couldn't guess whether she was angry, or upset, or what.

'If I can find it,' Mark grumbled. 'Probably crumpled up at the back of my wardrobe. Anyway, what's the point?'

'I'll be off now then. Cheerio! See you tomorrow, Mark.'

''Bye, Stewart.' Vanessa was pouring the eggs into heated butter in the pan. 'Oh, before you go, just tell me one thing.'

'What's that?' Tentatively, he reappeared in the doorway. Nervously, he shifted from one large foot to the other. Now what?

But Vanessa was beaming broadly at him. 'What *did* the elephant say to the naked man?'

CHAPTER THREE

MORNINGS were not Mark's best time of day, but this Friday he was all charm, even waking Vanessa with a cup of tea at seven forty-five. Half an hour later, tucking into a bowl of Wheat Flakes, he raised deep velvet-brown eyes and fixed them on her face. She loved them—loved him—so much, and not because those eyes were a mirror image of hers. Spreading marmalade on her toast, she smiled back.

'So, you won't reconsider, then?'

'Reconsider what?'

'You know what, Vanessa. Don't be...don't mess me about.'

She bit into the toast. 'No, Mark. I'm sorry.'

'What if I said I was doing it anyway? With Scully's backing?'

She sipped tea, to hide her flush of anger. 'You know you can't do that, Mark. You need my consent, whether you like it or not. And there's the headmaster too.'

'Oh, old Fergus couldn't care a damn what we do. If Scully tells him it's a good idea, he'll never...'

'All the same.' Vanessa was almost as sick of hearing about this Scully as she was of the great Seymour himself, the cause of all this upheaval. 'Now, can we drop the subject, please?'

For the moment, Mark complied. Ten minutes later, as he grabbed his coat in the hall, he tried one last time. 'Won't you even phone Mr Scully today? Or I could ask him to phone you, if you like.'

'No, I won't. I'll be busy today. I've got three orders on, and probably no proper transport. Just give it a rest, Mark. And get going, or you'll miss the bus, and I haven't got time to drive you to town.'

'Oh, OK, OK.' The charm was wearing thin. Mark managed a muttered 'cheers' as he slammed the front door and slouched off down the road, hands in pockets, ancient hessian satchel over one shoulder. The satchel had always been covered with scrawled graffiti—obscure private signs and symbols, the esoteric jargon of his generation—but Vanessa had never noticed before that the word 'Totem' appeared among them several times. She noticed it now, and it irritated her more than ever.

As the business of the day progressed, she was not allowed to forget it. Now the news was out, it swept the village like a tidal wave. Or perhaps half of them had known about it all along, but Vanessa had just been too preoccupied to pick up the gossip. She had never been a great one for listening to rumours. She had far too much to do.

Compton Magna was a lot less introverted and self-obsessed than some villages. It prided itself on being lively and outward-looking. But the fine old manor house, high up on its outskirts, had been empty much too long; and now to have someone so public coming there—so much part of all that was most modern, dashing, fast-moving—so metropolitan . . . so expensive . . .

Local opinion was split roughly down the middle. The disapprovers tended to be on the wrong side of forty. One of the few exceptions proving this rule was Vanessa. She resolved to have as little to do with the new arrivals as she could help.

The threat of their potential influence on her brother was bad enough. She had very different hopes and aspirations for him. But there was more to it than that: their presence felt menacing to Vanessa, personally. Since that unnerving encounter yesterday with the leader of the group—this Seymour, Public Hero Number One, whizz-kid on sixteen instruments, master of the widest range of musical styles—she had been all on edge, all unsettled.

All day, elbow-deep in raw ingredients and organisation, she seethed whenever she thought about it. God, the waste of talent! All that sensitivity— such opportunities at his disposal! How could anyone choose to use them that way, when he was free to do such . . .

For the umpteenth time she stopped work, folded her arms and shook her head. Immoral! Wicked! She must avoid the man, and everything he stood for, otherwise she wouldn't be accountable for her manners. By nature she was reticent, but when anything really upset her, she could suddenly become a firebrand. She hated it, she was ashamed of it, but occasionally she had no control over it.

Carol was still stuck at home with the ailing Johnny and her private problems. Kerry was still marooned in her isolated cottage, agitating about her beloved Gertrude, who had been hauled off to the garage for emergency surgery. Deprived of their normally reliable help and support, Vanessa was on the go from after breakfast till mid-evening.

The first task, when she finally arrived home, was to head for her small study at the back of the ground floor. Before the unwinding—the sherry and the soothing strains of Bach or Haydn or Mozart— there was still business to attend to. Every night, she followed the same routine. It was the only way to keep on top of life.

She sat at her desk, confronting the telephone. The wretched machine was not her favourite form of communication, but *Doorsteps* wouldn't have got far without it. In fact, her trade depended on it. Now she rewound the tape on her answerphone—another indispensable piece of modern technology—and sat, pen poised over pad, to see what demands the afternoon had brought her.

The first message was for Mark. Would he please ring Stephen, who was failing to make head or tail of this geography question? Mark always understood these things. Immediate assistance was urgently requested. Well, it would have to wait till Mark had finished his evening's homework. He was stuck into it, quietly for once—come to think of it she'd hardly seen him, but he'd been suspiciously calm and chatty when they'd had a quick cup of tea together earlier, hadn't mentioned Scully or Seymour or Totem at all, and Vanessa's mind had been elsewhere at the time...

She scribbled the message and pressed the button to continue the tape. A husky female voice hoped this was *Doorsteps* and wondered if it might be possible to put in a substantial order for Sunday.

Oh yes, it was possible. With *Doorsteps* all things had to be possible. With a sigh, Vanessa prepared to write down the details.

'It's for the old manor. You know, the big house on Beacon Hill?'

The voice was throaty and attractive, with strong London vowels, and Vanessa had never heard it before in her life. Before she realised what she was doing, a trembling finger had reached out to stop the tape. The manor house? Don't say she was being enlisted to feed a horde of raucous pop stars? And on a Sunday—they should be so lucky! She might need the business, but she wasn't *that* desperate.

Angry now, she punched the button again. Fancy implying that she might not know where the old manor was! Every resident in the village knew where it was. Only a crass newcomer, some city slicker, would be so condescending as to imagine...

'We've got engineers and builders in, doing our new studio,' the voice purred on. Its very femininity annoyed Vanessa. Rick Seymour's bit of stuff, no doubt, or one of them. What did they call them—groupies? Why couldn't they get some food together themselves? Or were they only good for one thing, as suggested in those sensationalist stories you read in the tabloid press?

'We've got to rehearse all day,' the voice was continuing. 'So we do hope you can manage a few snacks at least. If you can, could you ring us as soon as possible, please? Thanks ever so much.' She gave the number, then rang off.

Vanessa sat in silence as the machine bleeped, whirred and wound on through an empty tape. No more messages.

She switched it off, and went into the kitchen to put the kettle on. She was too tired to call them back this evening. In fact, she wasn't sure she was going to call them back at all. Why should she take the trouble to provide their weekend nourishment? Let them eat cake!

Early in the morning, she consulted Carol and Kerry. Their response was predictably emphatic: Vanessa was in a minority of one.

'There's no way we can afford to pick and choose our clients, or our days of the week.' Kerry sighed. 'But you'll have to take it in the car again, I'm afraid. Poor Gert won't be on the road till Monday. Mike told me last night that her transverse . . .'

'I'll cope,' Vanessa cut in, sparing herself the gory details.

'Tell you what though,' Kerry suggested. 'Get them to order flans and pasties, then I can make a batch of my special pastry and Charlie can run it down to Carol on his bike, and she can do some of her luscious fillings. All you'll have to do is get the stuff up there on Sunday.'

'Thanks, Kerry. I'll try and angle them that way.'

Carol, in her turn, became dreamy. 'I'd go with you like a shot.'

'It's OK, love, I can manage. You've got enough on your hands.'

'Oh, you'll manage; you always do. It wasn't that I was thinking of. I mean, Nessa—Rick Seymour! Have you ever seen him on TV?'

She had seen him a lot more closely than that, but she was keeping this information to herself, for obscure reasons. 'Carol, I won't be setting eyes on the illustrious Seymour, nor any of his cronies, with a bit of luck. I shall drop their order off at the door, and leave.'

Carol chuckled. 'Suppose it had been Simon Rattle, or the Amadeus String Quartet? You'd have crooned a different tune then!'

'How can you even imply they're in the same *league*?'

'Only teasing. Don't worry, I'll do them some of my special pasties. I should have time today; Johnny's on the mend. So, if you can fix it up with them, Vanessa, I think you should, Sunday or not. We can't really risk a reputation for turning down good trade, can we?'

'No, of course not. I'll get back to them straight away.'

Kerry and Carol were safe enough, stranded in their respective homes, leaving her to do the consumer relations bit—not that it usually caused her any problems. They weren't to know that this was one occasion when she found the whole idea alarming and irritating—and she had better reasons than they could understand. But they were right: business was business, and nothing should stand in its way.

She drummed her fingertips on the desk as she waited while the inhabitants of the manor house deigned to answer the telephone. Impatient thoughts ran through her head—hurry up... get a move on... I've got better things to do even if you haven't. What's the matter, no one out of bed at this hour?

'Manor house?'

Three syllables, cutting clear and sharp into her edgy musings. A male voice this time, and instantly familiar.

'Ah yes, hello.' Now she was flustered, and that made her all the more annoyed. '*Doorsteps* here. You left a message.'

'Doorsteps.' The pause was brief but expressive. Clearly, the word meant little to him. 'Sorry, Doorsteps, I can't place you. Are you booked to record this week? Have we got you on our schedule? If you'll just hang on a minute, I'll...'

Vanessa bristled. He was confusing her with some gang of caterwaulers, queuing up to use his facilities!

'I'm not a—a *group*! I'm a caterer. I received a message on my answerphone that you want food for tomorrow. Yes, I can supply it.'

'Ah...*Doorsteps*!' The mental click almost echoed down the line. 'Of course, I remember. I spotted your advertisement, and asked Ellie to ring, but I didn't realise she had. You can do us a few bits for tomorrow? You'll be saving our life, if so.'

Hardly *that* crucial, surely, not when you were as rich and successful as Rick Seymour?

Mind you, there was a certain genuine warmth in the voice, she had to admit that. Disembodied from the rest of him—from everything she knew about him—it was impossible not to respond to it. There was a quality of energy...vitality. More than a suggestion of that acute intelligence, the heightened artistic sensibility, the creativity. Vanessa cringed all over again. People with his gifts were so rare. How could he...?

'Are you still there, *Doorsteps*? Or have we been cut off in our prime?'

'I'm sorry. Yes, I'm still here. We can certainly do something tomorrow. Snacks, as your—colleague suggested, not a full-scale meal. Quiches, pasties, or an assortment of filled rolls. A few salads perhaps. Potato...coleslaw...'

If she could be clipped, so could he. 'That's the sort of thing, *Doorsteps*. Nourishing nibbles, a few sustaining sandwiches. No chips, though—something a bit healthier. My cohorts are into the wholefood scene. The high moral fibre, you know, the veggies that have lived a good life. The hand-knitted bread, the genuine homespun pastry. That's why I liked the look of your ad. "All organic local produce." Plenty of murky apple juice, crushed by rural feet, complete with pips and stalks.'

Vanessa grinned, but her tone was still terse. 'We do not offer chips. Not even french fries. I may be able to lay my hands on the odd carton of apple juice, but it would come from Sainsbury's. I could do you some smorgasbord—open sandwiches and...'

'I do happen to know what smorgasbord is. I recall that we much enjoyed it recently, in Malmö I think it was. I'm also rather partial to the Danish equivalent. Smørrebrød, I believe they call it? We had it in Copenhagen, several times. A sensual treat, like many of the excitements on offer in Copenhagen.'

He could mock all he liked; she didn't care if he rubbed her nose in his freedom—his sophisticated, cosmopolitan life-style. What did he know about her? He didn't even know who she was! As far as he was concerned, he was a remote idol—a pin-up; and she was an insignificant little purveyor of take-away food, whom he had never set eyes on in his life.

Fortified with this thought, Vanessa became even brisker. 'Right. We'll make you a selection of our wholemeal pastry range, with vegetarian fillings. For how many?'

'Oh, fourteen...fifteen should about cover it. Yes, call it fifteen hearty appetites. And can you bring it along about noon tomorrow? Or should one of us come and pick it up?'

'Delivery is part of our service, Mr Seymour. I shall have it ready my midday tomorrow.'

'On my doorstep.'

'Precisely.'

'But I'm sure your sandwiches are *never* door-steps, *Doorsteps*. Nothing so indelicate, so unsubtle.'

'Not unless the customers request them specially, no.'

'It's a clever name, though. I'll bet you thought it up yourself. I can tell by your voice, you're the sort of person who'd enjoy a good pun.'

The remark was straightforward—direct, uncomplicated. But Vanessa's response was as complex as any feeling she'd ever experienced. On the one hand, resentful. On the other, flattered. And she found herself rocking and weaving between the two like a roller-coaster.

'Funny thing,' he was drawling, before she could find a reply. 'You sound familiar. You don't sing, do you? Not leading a double life, Kate Bush in disguise?'

Even Vanessa had heard of Kate Bush. Some of her songs were not at all bad, to be honest. 'I lead a very ordinary life. No, I'm not—I don't—I'm not a singer.' She had gone stiff, all over, her knuckles white on the receiver. It was a struggle, not letting the stress through into her tone. He was just joking, chatting; if he only knew how deep they pierced, these innocent questions!

'Well, we've met before. I never forget a voice. Faces maybe, and names, all the time. I've got a head like a sieve for names, but voices, no.'

He was serious. His tone had a kind of strange determination: a persistence. He was going to find out, sooner or later, so it might as well be sooner. Vanessa braced herself, though she was scarcely sure exactly what for.

'We met in the church, on Thursday. You were playing the organ.'

'Good God!' he swore appropriately. 'Of course!' There was a short, sharp pause. 'In this instance,' he went on, more softly, 'I haven't forgotten the face, either, or the rest of you, come to that. I can't have forgotten your name, because I'm pretty sure

you never divulged it.' There was another pause.
If he was waiting for her to divulge it now, Vanessa
did not oblige. 'Once again, you have me at a disadvantage, *Doorsteps*, since you're clearly aware
of mine.'

'I am—now.' Vanessa fought down this churning
blend of hostility and heat, and her voice emerged
starchier than ever. 'I wasn't then.'

'Not one of my ardent fans?'

'There *are* a few of us left. I don't actually follow
the—pop scene.' Ice positively dripped from the
phrase. Vanessa couldn't help it. The words were
more than a simple statement; they were a way of
life.

'Prefer César Franck, eh?' He chuckled, not in
the least put out. 'Well, each to his own. I beg your
pardon, *her* own. I realise not everyone shares my
entirely catholic tastes in music.'

'Quite.' Enough about that. Least said, soonest
forgotten. 'Now, I must get on with your order, Mr
Seymour, if you'll...'

'Hey, listen, *Doorsteps*. Defrost a minute, will
you? You're giving me chilblains.'

'Pardon?'

'Rick. The name is Rick. Consider my image!
Think of my reputation! My public would desert
me in droves! All this Seymour bit—it's not me at
all,' he complained.

'But...'

'Look, we're obviously destined to be neigh-
bours, whether you like it—or me—or my music,
or not. And what's more,' he added, on a conspira-
torial note, 'if this shower up here likes your
goodies, it certainly won't be the last time your
catering services are called on. It could be good for
business, you know what I mean? So, if you can

force yourself to descend to such dangerous intimacy, I do much prefer to be known as Rick.'

'But . . .'

'Afraid it's not proper? An outrage to your professional conduct?'

'Well, there is that, yes.' And more.

'Fair enough.' He seemed remarkably serious, in his flippant way, about this whole subject. 'How about a compromise? I was christened Richard. Is that better? Perhaps more in keeping with the Bach toccatas? Or more fitting for the ceremonial exchange of quiche and pasty?'

'If you insist.' Really, this was stupid. They'd only met once, and that was by accident, and if Vanessa had any say in the matter, any future contact would be at a purely commercial level, so . . .

'I do. So, what do I call you? I can hardly go on addressing you as *Doorsteps*. It lacks that human touch. People don't generally call me Totem.'

'Davies,' Vanessa informed him breezily.

'Ms Davies?'

'Miss Davies. Yes.'

'With an e?'

'That's right. The Welsh way.'

She waited for some wry comment, but all she got was a thoughtful, 'Hmmm.' After a brief pause, he went on, 'That's another funny thing. I know you didn't tell me on Thursday, but even your name rings a bell. I've heard it somewhere recently, I know I have.'

'Every fourth family in Wales is called Davies. It's not exactly . . .'

'No, but there's something else, quite specific. I can't place it.'

'Nothing to do with me,' Vanessa assured him roundly. She felt less confident than she sounded.

There was no chance, was there, that this infuriating business about Mark and the work experience
had already reached the ears of the great man
himself? And even if it had, surely someone as busy
as Rick Seymour would never remember such a
detail?

'No, I don't suppose so,' he was saying, and she
relaxed. 'Some agent, I expect, or technician, or
the man who came to see to the PA system, or one
of the band's second cousins pestering for an
audition.'

He sounded suddenly weary. In that moment,
Vanessa understood that life wasn't all glory and
roses, standing where he stood, in that relentless
public spotlight. Not that he had anyone to blame
but himself. 'Probably.' She seized on his expla-
nations with relief. 'Now, I've really got to get on,
Mr Seymour, if that's all . . .'

'Who?'

She sighed. 'Richard.' His intuition had been un-
cannily accurate; it was easier to say Richard than
Rick.

'OK, Miss Davies.'

The implication was clear, but if he wanted to
know more, he could whistle. For a routine
booking, this was ridiculously convoluted.

'I'll bring the account when I come, shall I? Or
would you like me to get back to you today with a
cost quote?'

'Oh, bring the bill in the morning. Money is no
object, that's the least of our worries.' Yes, well,
it would be. 'Just feed the five thousand, that's all
we're bothered about. It'll be cash,' he added, 'no
problem.'

This whole affair was no problem to anyone, it
seemed. So why should it be to Vanessa?

'I'll be there. It's no miracle; it's what we're here for,' she pointed out, acidly.

'Will you be bringing the goodies yourself? Don't you employ a brawny driver to shift them around, or do you want to borrow one of my roadies? You should see the biceps on some of these guys!'

'Our van's off sick, as it happens. But I can manage fine, thanks.' Anyway, biceps aren't really my thing. Never have been, she added to herself. 'Actually,' she smiled, just slightly, 'I wouldn't describe our usual driver as brawny, exactly.'

'Not the muscular type? You don't go for the macho effect?'

Frivolous banter—but probing, between the lines, as Vanessa well knew. *Is there a man in your life?* It happened all the time, and it never failed to irritate Vanessa. What difference did it make to anything, whether she was single, or attached, or what? Why couldn't people see her as an individual, without categorising her?

'I don't make generalisations, about that or anything else. And as for our usual driver, I'd say she was on the petite side,' she added, with a hint of mischief.

'*Touché.*' She could hear the grin in his voice. He was not in the least abashed. 'An all-woman outfit, eh? Very commendable.'

'Thank *you*!' She was deeply sarcastic. Talk about patronising!

'Think nothing of it, Miss Davies. We'll expect you tomorrow, then?'

'Midday. I'll be there.'

'Could you go round to the kitchen door, please? It's at the back.'

'Tradesmen's entrance?'

'Naturally. Where else? Or should we say tradespersons?'

'I don't happen to believe equality is about what words we use.'

'As a matter of fact, neither do I.' His tone was surprisingly low and level.

'Goodbye then. If I don't chase my colleagues up now, you won't get your pasties and things at all.'

'That would be a disaster. The collapse of important studio sessions. If you knew what they get like when they're hungry! Animals, these rocksters. They'd dismember the equipment, chew on the carpet.'

'I can imagine.' He might be digging at her prejudices, but Vanessa could believe it only too literally.

'Then there's the drugs, of course. If you don't feed 'em, you never know what noxious substances they'll take refuge in.'

He was really satirising her now, but she refused to rise to it. She was paying for this call, for heaven's sake! 'I won't let you down.'

'Perish the thought, Miss Davies. Oh, by the way, I nearly forgot.'

'Yes?' She held the receiver away from her ear, so that she could look at her wristwatch.

'Did you find your friend's ring?'

'Oh. Yes, I did, straight away. It was very lucky.'

'That's good news. My performance must have inspired you.'

It had been an inspiring performance, sure enough. But if he was fishing for compliments, he had chosen the wrong river. 'I knew where it was likely to be, and it was,' she declared coolly.

'Clever old you. Well, thanks for calling, Miss Davies. We do appreciate this, specially on a Sunday. 'Bye for now.'

His turn to become brisk. 'Goodbye,' she said. But the line was already buzzing emptily. It had been an unexpected, cryptic conversation. Now it was over, and she had a mound of organising to do, as usual.

CHAPTER FOUR

THE old manor house stood in its traditional setting, dating from the days when it had carried out a traditional village role—strong, dominant, set slightly apart and raised. Originally Tudor, it had been extended and renovated at roughly hundred-year intervals. The result, rather than a jumble of styles, was a harmonious whole, full of character. Quietly dignified in its own rolling green estate; commanding wide views of countryside, stretching to a hazy coastline.

Turning her car in through open wrought-iron gates and up the sweep of drive, Vanessa reflected that the last of these additions had probably happened just about a century ago, with the Victorian banqueting hall. So the place must be due for its next spate of attention. Apart from basic modernisation, the last owners had hardly touched it before packing up and emigrating to Canada. Since then it had waited for that rare being with enough vision, energy, motivation, and above all money, to take it in hand.

This person had evidently materialised at last, in the unorthodox form of contemporary celebrity, Rick Seymour. And who could be more fitting to initiate these latest improvements—if it could be called an improvement, dragging the fine old building kicking and screaming into the third millenium?

Vanessa drove smartly round the back, as instructed, and parked in the wide, cobbled stable yard, alongside a motley selection of rural Range Rovers, pretentious BMWs, flashy sports cars, battered jalopies, sensible estate vehicles, and a full-sized—apparently fully furnished—blue double-decker bus. Not to mention the posse of hairy two-wheeled machines which would have brought cries of envious joy from Mark and Stewart and their cronies—as well as Kerry's Charlie, a motorcycle fanatic.

It was exactly noon when she stood at the back door, clutching the first of several boxes of carefully wrapped goodies. Outwardly, she was cool and efficient, in cream cords, and a chunky cable-knit tan jacket. Inwardly, she fluttered with nervous tension, sparring with a degree of determination. The moment this lot had safely changed hands—and the money too, of course—she was off. They could unwrap them, warm them up, sort them out without benefit of her guidance.

The old-fashioned bell jangled hollowly through the house. Vanessa half-expected to confront a maid, complete with frilly apron, or a severe butler, or uniformed footman. This place had a very special atmosphere, and always had everyone said so. Vanessa had only set foot in it two or three times in all these years, but the vibes were interesting—welcoming, yet oddly penetrating, as if the old walls had seen it all before, and nothing would surprise them, and you might as well just act naturally because in here, you wouldn't get away with anything less . . .

The person now greeting her was branded with the unmistakable aura, the uncompromising image

of the nineteen-eighties. Dressed in loose layers of
vivid prints—baggy trousers, flowing shirt, tunic—
all designed to clash rather than match, but to do
it in high style. Black frizz of hair beaded into a
myriad of cheerful colours. Scarlet-striped espa-
drilles; scatterings of silver glitter on smooth ebony
cheeks and forehead.

She was West Indian, and stunning. One of the
most striking women Vanessa had ever seen. Now
she smiled broadly, and Vanessa decided she was
also one of the most beautiful.

'Hello there! You must be...'

'*Doorsteps.*' Vanessa hoisted the box up under
her arm, trying hard not to stare too blatantly.

'Right. That's marvellous! We're so grateful,
you've no idea. We do have this really helpful
lady—she comes on weekdays, cleans and tidies and
that—but as far as cooking goes we're on our own,
and none of us is much good at it, so we haven't
sorted ourselves out yet.'

Definitely those same rich London tones which
had regaled Vanessa's answerphone, only its owner
did not resemble Vanessa's preconceptions of a
groupie, or any kind of cheap hanger-on. She was
poised, mature and relaxed—and spontaneously
friendly.

Vanessa was suffering from a coldly uncomfortable sensation which she recognised as a crumbling
of rooted prejudices.

'It's quite OK. No trouble, as I explained.'

'Rick told me what you said. We can't wait to
try these pasties and pies and things. They sound
fantastic. Here, come on, let me give you a hand.
More stuff in the car, is there?'

She reached out to take the box from Vanessa.
Tapering fingers closed around it, festooned with
rings; and among them, a thick gold band on the
third finger of her left hand. Another pre-
judgement biting the dust: whatever role she played
in this group, here was a confident married woman,
not some frivolous floozie.

'Rick's organising the rehearsal sessions, but he
said he'd be down and help when you arrived. OK,
I've got this: you can let go.'

'Oh, there's no need for that. None of it's heavy,
we can easily...'

But it was too late for protest. As if the girl had
conjured him up, Rick Seymour appeared, prompt
on cue, in the hallway behind her.

His slim jeans and crisp cotton shirt seemed
positively bland and ordinary, in contrast to all her
vibrant splendour. The piercing blue eyes—those
sharp features, the acute expression—did not. Nor
did the extraordinary warmth which emanated from
him as he came up to the girl and placed both hands
on her shoulders, to regard Vanessa over the top
of the beaded black head.

Yes, he had something—she supposed it might
be called star quality in the glossies—charisma
perhaps, or sheer magnetism? If it was as clear as
this, standing here on the threshold in his shirtsleeves on a Sunday morning, what must it be like
when he held a stage, or a screen, or a stadium?

Vanessa stared back at him, much too preoccupied with her thoughts to feel embarrassed. Just
imagine it, all directed into a classical recital on the
organ, or some superb Bechstein Grand...or she
could envisage him as a conductor, manipulating a

whole orchestra with the subtlest wave of his baton...

'We meet again,' he was saying. 'Miss Davies, may I introduce Ms Dale? Without whom, life around here would be null and void,' he declared dramatically. 'The caffeine in our coffee, the tannin in our tea,' he rhapsodised. 'The salt in our stew, the...'

'For God's sake, Rick!' But the girl's smile widened as she dealt him a nifty dig in the ribs, with a backward slant of her elbow. 'I'm Ellie,' she told Vanessa. 'Don't listen to him.'

Rick dodged the jab with practised ease. 'And this is Miss Davies, Ellie, but you can call her Doorsteps.'

On the telephone, this gibe had been cutting enough. In the flesh, it was unassailable. Vanessa's armour dissolved; she even smiled.

'My name is Vanessa.'

'Vanessa. Vanessa Davies. Miss Vanessa Doorsteps Davies.' He rolled it around his tongue, savouring it. He had a very lyrical voice: low, meditative, with an impact which cut through to the nerve-centres, without need of volume, let alone artificial sound production. All done by quality, rather than quantity. Vanessa knew a thing or two about the human voice, and she recognized the outstanding when she heard it. All the more galling, then, that...

'Very nice too,' he was observing. 'Very sweet. Very sedate.'

He was still studying her, so intently she thought he must see right through her and out the other side. And there was a hint of something darker than simple curiosity, too: a suggestion of hostility.

Before Vanessa could speak, Ellie had turned round, close against him, face to face, and shoved the box into his arms. 'Here, you, make yourself useful. We haven't got all day, and neither has Vanessa. She's given up half her weekend for us and our greedy appetites as it is, so move it, Seymour.'

Vanessa watched and listened, thrust out on a limb, as the pair of them shared one of those quick, timeless glances known only to secure, close, trusted friends. Lovers? She understood, in a flash, what she should have realised minutes ago. These two *were* a couple. Husband and wife, no less, if Ellie's ring was anything to judge by! She felt even more foolish and, unaccountably, painfully chilled and empty.

Three seconds later, Rick had disappeared into the kitchen with the box and Ellie was helping Vanessa unload the rest from her car and carry them into the house. If she had expected unpleasant din, or sordid chaos—the disreputable trappings of a stereotyped pop life-style—she was wrong. The atmosphere was exceptionally peaceful. The huge kitchen was clean, tidy, airy and well equipped.

She gazed around. Rick had temporarily vanished, no doubt to supervise the hungry hordes, wherever they were. She hoped he'd get waylaid, then she could make her escape. Surely Ellie could give her the money; not that it really mattered, she could easily send them a bill.

Ellie closed the door by leaning back against it, then dumped the last box on the scrubbed pine refectory table. There was more than enough room to sit and feed the fifteen Vanessa had catered for. But where were they?

Perhaps guessing her thoughts, Ellie grinned.
'Quiet, huh? First thing we had done was complete
insulation for noise. Every studio has to be totally
sound-proofed. Recording, rehearsing—whatever
you're doing it's essential. Especially if you're living
in the place as well. There's nothing worse than not
being able to get away from the work.'

'Or having everyday life intruding on it when you
need to concentrate.' Vanessa had wandered over
to the window; now she turned to face Ellie.

'Right.' Ellie's smile was so wide and natural, it
was impossible not to relax and return it. 'Hey, you
obviously understand all about it. Do you like
music? Or play anything yourself?'

'Oh yes, I love music, but not your kind.' The
words were out before she could modify them, yet
why should she want to? Usually she felt only too
ready to deny the slightest hint of instrinsic value
in popular music. But somehow here, today, the
bare statement sounded churlish, even in her own
ears. Instead of proud, she felt almost apologetic.

Ellie was still looking at her, a genuine warmth
of interest in her eyes. 'What kind, then?'

'I do... I did... well, I did used to sing. Once.'

Good grief! What in the name of heaven had in-
duced her to come out with that revelation? Just
like that—as a simple fact, without any layers of
tormented regret! She never, *never* spoke about this,
but now it had slipped out, unpremeditated, to a
total stranger who surely couldn't even begin to appreciate its significance.

Ellie seemed to take it in her stride. 'Really?
That's great! See, we're two of a kind—birds of a
feather, eh? I knew I liked you, as soon as I saw
you! So, what did you sing and why did you stop?'

'Oh, it didn't—it came to nothing, really. I mean, I never...'

Ellie was not in the least fazed by Vanessa's incoherent mumbles. 'I expect it was classical stuff?'

'That's right. I didn't get very far, but...'

'Yeah, I thought it would be. Rick told me about your meeting in the church. It must have been a laugh, stumbling across him like that!'

'Oh, he told you, did he?' He was bound to tell her everything that happened to him, if they were the close couple they appeared to be. 'Yes, well, that's right. Classical. Choral work, and some amateur operatics, but I never really got round to...'

'It's not so different from my sort of stuff, you know, Vanessa.' Ellie was still smiling, but her tone had grown intense. 'Not when you really listen and feel it. Dig deep down for what it's all about. Music's a universal church. All art is. That's what I believe, and so does Rick.'

'So I gathered.' Vanessa became wry, recalling those hands of his, mastering the organ keys, creating those breathtaking cadences. 'Do you sing too, then?'

Even as she phrased the question, Rick himself sauntered in. How did he manage to look as if he had all the time in the world, when he must be under constant pressure?

'Does she sing? Does this little nightingale *sing*? Did I hear you right, Miss Davies?'

'Well, I...'

She had evidently committed a major *faux pas*, but Ellie was chuckling happily. 'Refreshing, I call it. Finding someone who couldn't give a damn about Totem, doesn't even know our line-up. Why the hell should she know, anyway? She's not into our sort of sounds. You know that as well as I do, Rick.' Another of those exchanged glances, full of instant meaning. 'And what's more, she's just been telling me, she used to do a bit of singing herself.'

This was sinking from the ridiculous to the preposterous. 'No, really, I only...'

But Rick was surveying her with a new expression of detached speculation. 'Is that so? I wondered what your thing was.'

'It was never my—*thing*. Just that I once hoped...'

But Rick was strolling over to where Ellie stood, then winding an arm around her waist. Together, the one so dark, the other so fair, they continued to inspect Vanessa. 'Well, in that case, all the more reason why you should know that Ellie is the main vocalist of Totem. She belts it out like no one else in the business. Pop or classical,' he added, with profound emphasis. 'Moves like a dream, too, when we do our stage act. She's the lynch-pin of the whole outfit, really. Audiences rave about her. All of us love her.' He drew Ellie closer, smiling down at her. Then he was staring straight at Vanessa again. 'Surprises you, does it?' The smile had faded.

Vanessa's throat felt rough and dry. 'No, of course not! I just didn't realise, that's all. I thought *you* were the lead singer. As I told you, I hardly know anything about it!'

She'd quite forgotten to nag Mark about showing her that poster of the group. Pity—seeing it again, she'd easily have remembered them both, in context. Turning from Rick to Ellie, her defiance gave way to a sincere apology. 'No offence, Ellie. I'm sure you're—you're great; it's just that I——'

'Despise the medium?' Rick was quick to cut in.

But Ellie broke from his fond grasp, walked over to Vanessa and took her hand. The gesture was so unexpected, and yet so natural, it paralysed Vanessa completely.

'I've told you, Vanessa, it's nothing. Rick's exaggerating; he always does. He sings as much as I do. We often take vocal lines together, as it happens. It's just that he does everything else as well, including writing the songs, and all I can do is perform them. Anyway,' she grinned again, 'I also told you, I *like* the idea of not being recognised by someone, not even known about. It's such a drag, having no private life. You can come over and see me any time, Vanessa. Maybe we could try out a few numbers together?'

'Numbers?' Vanessa frowned, then blushed, but she did not withdraw her hand. 'Oh, I see. Well, I don't know...'

'Miss Davies wouldn't want to do that, Ellie. I hate to break up this tender scene, but maybe you need to be reminded that she doesn't just dislike our sort of music; she disapproves of it. She thinks it's nasty evil stuff, beneath her dignity, and especially harmful to the young, impressionable ear and mind.'

From terse objectivity, his tone had hardened to outright bitterness. Now Vanessa's hand broke from Ellie's, as both women wheeled on him.

'*No*, Rick!' Ellie's face was solemn, and her voice held a clear warning. 'You promised you wouldn't!'

'It's not *like* that!' So, he did know about Mark, after all! Now her worst fears were confirmed, Vanessa grew shrill. 'You don't know anything about it!'

'So what *is* it like?' He was ignoring Ellie, fixing all his attention on Vanessa's flushed face. 'Maybe you could explain?'

'Why should I? It's none of your business!'

She wasn't just confused. She was furious, that this trivial, entirely personal disagreement between Mark and herself had become public property.

'If it's not my business, I'd like to know whose it is.' He matched her agitation with coldness. 'I get asked this great favour by a mate of mine, someone I don't even know all that well, who I've met through the trade. This young lad, he says, dead keen, lives and breathes rock music. Needs something to do for—what did I say he called it?' he broke off to appeal to Ellie. 'Work experience, that was it. Great idea, I remember thinking—wish we'd had anything so civilised when I was at school. Anyway, so this guy, Ron Scully, tells me it'll make the boy's life worth living if he can only spend a couple of days sitting in with the group. No matter what we're doing, he says. Playing, rehearsing, just being—if he could absorb a bit of our atmosphere, see some of our methods, get an inside view...'

The ice was melting now, but the intense irritation replacing it was even more alarming. Vanessa backed away, but Ellie crossed to him. 'Rick,' she pleaded. 'This is silly! You know what we...'

He shook her hand from his arm. 'So here we are, apparently in this young fellow's actual village. And I do owe Ron a favour. He was good to us, way back when we used to do pub gigs in Bristol— a good PR contact. And when we played the Colston Hall recently, he alerted the local press in all sorts of obscure places. So, I said, why not? It's the first time in my life I've ever agreed to any such thing. If I let 'em all come,' he snarled at Vanessa, as if she was personally responsible for every clamouring fan in his life, 'if I even let one in every thousand come, I'd be buried alive. The flesh picked clean from the bones.'

'Oh, Rick!' Ellie knew him of old. She had given up arguing and now stood aside, sighing, shaking her head and casting rueful glances at him and Vanessa in turn.

'Well,' he challenged, 'it's true, isn't it? Isn't it, Ellie?'

'OK, OK. It's true, it's true!'

'I really don't see why it has to upset you so much.' Vanessa saw her chance to get a word in edgeways—and defuse his mounting tension, which was like a physical force, suffocating her. She hated scenes, temperamental clashes, more than anything. If sweet reason would deal with a situation, it ought to be given the chance. 'I mean, you must be so busy. Why should you *want* to take the trouble to enlighten a besotted sixteen-year old? It was good of this—Scully, having the idea, but he hasn't been at the school long, and music isn't even one of Mark's O-level subjects. He's got his exams in a few months; he hasn't got time to waste now, indulging in fantasies about...'

The attempt at reason had been doomed from the start. Rick boiled over. 'Fantasy? Who said anything about fantasy? Who gave *you* the right to judge what's real and what isn't? What kind of arrogant elitist *are* you? Just because your notion of what constitutes *real* music, *real* art, doesn't tally with everyone's...'

'Just hold it there, you two.' Ellie, stepping into her referee's role, held out a hand to each of them, restraining, separating. 'OK, so I can see we're not going to avoid this thing being well and truly aired. I'm sorry, Vanessa.' The brown eyes were soft, but the tone was firm. 'I thought we'd agreed we wouldn't say anything today. After Rick had the phone call last night, and put two and two together—realised who you were—he wanted to get back to you straight away, but I persuaded him it wasn't worth it.'

Rick interrupted the peace-keeping efforts with a minor explosion, somewhere between a snort and a sneer, but he suffered Ellie to go on.

'Ron rang to explain that your brother wouldn't be allowed to come after all. He didn't say much, just that there was this elder sister who was responsible for him, and she was against the idea because of not liking pop music.'

Ellie waited, while Rick and Vanessa glared at each other. 'How did you know it was me?' Vanessa finally muttered.

'I already knew your surname, from when he first asked me. Yesterday he told me a bit more about you, said you ran this catering service in the village. I couldn't really be in any doubt after that, could I?'

Rick had hooked his thumbs into the waistband of his jeans. Every angle of him exuded controlled annoyance.

'What I'd like to know, Vanessa, is why you have to take such decisions at all? I mean, you must be younger than *me*, for God's sake! Are your parents abroad, or what?' Ellie was gentle, but candidly curious. Without looking at him—instinctively—Vanessa could feel Rick's blue eyes watching for her reaction.

She stared down at her feet, then out of the window. This time the silence was so dense, you could have cut it with a blunt blade.

Suddenly, she stopped fidgeting and stared straight into their eyes: Ellie's attentive ones, Rick's quizzical ones. And then, for once, she opened her mouth and let the words out—let them take care of themselves.

'We haven't got any parents. They died, in a road accident, five years ago. A multiple pile-up on the M5, in fog. Just north of Taunton.' She blurted the information out, into a shocked silence.

'Bloody hell!' Ellie was the first to leap into action. Her two palms jerked up, pressing her cheeks. Her eyes rolled upwards, and her tone rose to a shriek, as pity and horror poured from her. 'You poor, *poor* girl! You poor kids! That's just so—cruel! No one else—in the family, I mean?'

In the face of Ellie's spontaneous outburst of pure sympathy, Vanessa bridled, then rallied. She was used to it, after all. 'Not really. Two grand-parents were dead, and the other two ailing. But we managed.' She was dignified, defiant as always; but the break in her voice was not lost on either of her listeners.

'So how old were you when this happened, Vanessa?' Rick had released his angry frustration, but still watched her, absorbed, yet dispassionate. 'It was five years ago, you said?'

'Eighteen: just leaving school.' There was no point in prevaricating. If they were determined to prise all this out of her, they might as well have the gory details. 'Perfectly capable of making my way. *Our* way.'

'Just about to go on to higher things in the world?'

'How do you mean?' Her fists were clenched, though she hardly knew it.

'Some kind of higher education, perhaps?'

'Perhaps,' she admitted, with a slight shrug. *So what?*

'Training, maybe?' he persisted. The blue eyes never left hers.

'Maybe. I—I hadn't quite decided. Not then.'

Now her gaze dropped. She reached up to brush the long fringe from her hot forehead. It really was very hot. She felt quite sticky. Oppressed... Breathless...

Enough of this! How had a routine delivery of an order deteriorated into all this? Air—she must get out into the air! Lots of it, and quickly. She moved towards the door—and swayed. She clutched the nearest object, which happened to be Ellie's shoulder, and collapsed into a kitchen chair. The room spun, righted itself, then hazed and wavered behind a mask of tears.

They ran down her face, into her mouth. They were a relief, but such a humiliation! The shame, the weakness! And here, with these, of all people, whom she barely knew, and cared about still less!

Ellie was in full charge, clucking and chirruping over her like a mother hen.

'*Now* see what you've been and gone and done!' Presumably this was aimed at Rick. Vanessa was too exhausted to notice. 'You've really upset her now!'

'It wasn't me who asked about her parents,' Rick pointed out calmly.

'All the same...' Ellie's arm was around Vanessa, her hand stroking the clammy brow. 'It's OK,

Vanessa. Not to worry. We'll make you a nice cup of coffee, then you must...'

'Glass of brandy might be nearer the mark.' There was a genuine concern under Rick's sardonic note.

Vanessa was recovering rapidly. 'No, no—just the coffee. Black, please. I didn't have any breakfast, must be empty or something—don't know what came over me...'

'You'll stay and have one of your own pasties. I'm not letting you loose on the roads in this condition. What about your brother? Will he be worried? Should you phone him?' Ellie was bustling now, filling the kettle.

'Oh no, he won't worry. He's not even at home today, he's gone to a friend's. They're revising for their exams together.' And playing their electric guitars, no doubt, she added to herself.

'Right then.' It was Rick's turn to step into command. 'I'll tell you exactly what we're going to do. Any second now, the gang's going to be down here, bellyaching for their lunch.'

Ellie looked at the clock, and squeaked. 'Oh, my Gawd, it's after one! They should be here already, and we haven't...'

'Right, so get these things unpacked and in the oven, El. Vanessa and I will repair to my office, where we shall enjoy a quiet cup of coffee, without slanging each other, and I shall settle my bill. And then, when she feels quite restored and ready, she can go home.'

'I feel quite restored and ready now,' Vanessa lied. 'I'll just...'

But from upstairs came the sound of heavy footsteps clumping; voices calling, laughing, singing.

There was a clattering of shoes on bare floorboards, slamming doors. Several floors, halls, cor-
ridors away as yet, but definitely heading this way.
Definitely the approach of a party of overworked,
underfed musicians and technicians. Definitely the
last prospect Vanessa felt like confronting at this
moment.

'All right, then.' She staggered to her feet, turning
to Rick. 'It doesn't matter about the money, but if
I could just wait somewhere quiet for a few
minutes—maybe use your bathroom...'

'Of course, and I'll fend this lot off. Don't worry
about a thing.' Ellie hustled her to the kitchen door.
'You look after her, Rick, OK? And just behave
yourself this time. If you'd listened to me before,
none of this would have happened.'

'Sorry, boss.' Rick stepped ahead to open the
door for Vanessa. He looked far from remorseful,
but at least he'd calmed down; that irrational an-
tagonism had receded as fast as it had surged. 'You
know what my temper's like. You know how
strongly I feel about—certain things.'

'Course I do. That's why I warned you, idiot!'

Again the mutual glance, the swift half-smile.
Even in her present state, Vanessa registered it, and
now she knew she resented it. She had slipped down
some slope, out of emotional control, and all sorts
of crazy shifts were happening in her head.

Externally she was composed now, and dry-eyed,
as she followed Rick out into the corridor. 'I'll bring
you the coffee in a minute!' Ellie called after them.
'You have a nice wash, Vanessa. You'll feel much
better if you splash your face.'

The noises off grew nearer, less muffled. Rick led her round a corner, across an empty hallway, past several doors.

'Here's the bathroom. Help yourself.' He pointed. 'No one intrudes on my working area, except by invitation, of course.'

'I'm honoured.' She managed a tinge of irony, if only on a murmur. 'Mustn't trespass on your hospitality too long...just so that I can get myself together...'

'No question of trespass—you were invited, remember?' There, in that stark, narrow passage, he stepped closer to her, and for the first time he really smiled, from the eyes. Vanessa had no choice: she smiled back. 'And if you need getting together, it's my fault as much as anyone's.'

Why was she trembling? At this unexpectedly direct gentleness in his tone? Or the physical sensation of him only inches away?

'Vanessa,' he went on, more urgently, 'I didn't want you to leave before hearing something—before I had the chance to explain one thing that might make it easier to understand why I got so hassled, and so hard on you.'

'It really doesn't matter,' she mumbled. 'I didn't mind.'

'Yes, it does, and yes, you did. I can't leave it like that. I don't like to let feelings fester. If I've got to have anything out, I like to do it straight away. It's how I work.'

'You don't say!' Hands in pockets, she faced him squarely.

He smiled again. 'Cloakroom?' He repeated the invitation, with a nod towards the door.

'Oh, yes. Thanks.'

'I'm sure you'll meet the mob one day, but not now, I think?'

'Will I?' *Not if I see them first!*

'Why not?'

He flung the remark over his shoulder, heading for his office. She ducked into the neat washroom—freshly painted, smelling of soap and spicy after-shave. She splashed her face, then studied it, expressionlessly, in the mirror. Finally she turned smartly on her heel, leaving her reflection behind.

CHAPTER FIVE

VANESSA arrived at Rick's office door just as Ellie was shoving the coffee tray through it, complete with earthenware mugs, milk jug, sugar bowl, and a plate of bourbon biscuits and ginger nuts. The aromatic steam rose, strong and freshly ground. Vanessa had seldom needed anything so much. As for the rest of this interview—whatever obscure matters Rick wanted to raise with her—she was balancing between apprehension and anticipation, reaching a pivot of surprising poise somewhere at the centre.

Ellie stayed long enough to grin broadly, and make sure the tray was safe in Rick's capable hands, then retreated to the kitchen regions where the converging crowd was vociferously making its demands known.

'Hey, where's this grub, then? I'm rumbling, man!'

'Put the kettle on, someone! If I don't get a fix of caffeine in twenty seconds flat, it'll be intravenous drip time.'

'Ellie! Rick! For God's sake, where *are* you?'

'What's in this oven? These smells are killing me!'

'Isn't the stuff ready yet? I think I'm dying of malnutrition.'

Rick returned Ellie's grin as she backed off to deal with the insurrection. 'Can you cope all right out there? It sounds as if they're about to eat each other.'

'Of course we can. We're not stupid, and anyhow, if we get into problems, we know where to locate the expert, don't we?'

Vanessa smiled back, but Rick held up a warning hand. '*Doorsteps* have fulfilled their contract, Ellie. The last thing Vanessa needs now is having to sort out a pile of pasties for a troupe of drooling engineers and instrumentalists. If you want help, give *me* a call, OK?'

'Don't be silly, I was only joking. Of course we'll manage. Gid promised to help, and he should be down by now. Relax, both of you, hang loose. Take your time, Vanessa.'

Vanessa stared at the closed door, slightly bemused. 'Gid?'

'Our saxophonist, Gideon. Sorry—I forget you don't know these details.'

'Unlike everyone else in the world, you mean? No, I didn't realise your group included—er—a brass section.'

'A brass section, eh? I'm not sure Gid quite classes it in that category. You wait till you hear what he does with it. Makes the greatest sounds on tenor and alto around.' Rick turned away to organise the coffee. 'He's also a great guy and a good organiser; he'll soon have them all under control. They make a good team. Black, wasn't it? Sugar?'

'Oh ... no, thanks. Just as it is.'

'Help yourself, then, and take a biscuit. Take three biscuits—and do sit down, Vanessa. Don't hover in that corner—this isn't just the end of round one. I've put my boxing gloves away. You won't need a fast escape route, either; you can leave whenever you like. I think you'll find I'm fairly docile, once you get to know me. What's more, I had these plush armchairs imported specially, so don't insult me by rejecting them.'

He perched on the side of his desk, cradling his coffee mug. Vanessa obeyed his instructions. Ten minutes ago, it had seemed logical, agreeing to take sanctuary in here—a brief respite, a simple patching over of differences. Now, she was beginning to wish she'd made a dash for freedom.

Evading Rick's eyes, she gazed around the room. It was compact, orderly, efficient, with filing cabinets, telephones, desk diaries. Not the sort of atmosphere she associated with rock bands.

'It's a very nice office. Very comfortable chairs.'

Rick was even more sardonic. 'What did you expect? Anarchy, instant gratification? We're just ordinary humans, you know, like the rest of you. Need places to work, places to play, places to do all our various things.'

'Of course, but . . .'

'A private office is absolutely indispensable. First priority, along with the studios. I need somewhere to think, write, keep up with the paperwork. Confirming bookings, liaising with contacts, all that sort of thing.'

Vanessa was taken aback. 'Don't you have a manager to take care of those arrangements? I thought all groups did, especially if they're as well known as you?'

'You thought right. Most bands do have managers, and most managers get fat on the proceeds. OK, so they take some of the administrative pressure off, so the musicians can concentrate on getting out there and performing. We have an agent in London who does a good job with PR and some scheduling. But basically, I prefer to keep hold of the reins myself.' His tone hardened. 'I'm perfectly capable of running this show. I don't intend to abdicate any of the responsibility—and I do mean *any*—unless I'm forced to.'

Vanessa sipped her coffee and crunched into a second ginger nut. Her confidence was flowing back. Perhaps it was the sustenance; or perhaps it was an infection from Rick's characteristic vehemence.

'When you say responsibility,' she ventured, 'don't you mean power?'

She met his eyes boldly, and he smiled. 'Shall we settle for control? If you're accusing me of running some kind of one-man dictatorship here, you can think again. This is a democracy, all down the line. We function on a co-operative basis, musically and otherwise. We practise, discuss, reach decisions together, as a group. But someone has to have the final say, Vanessa. You must know all about that, in your business.'

'Someone has to take the responsibility, yes.'

'I initiated this whole thing; I got our act together. We work well, as a band, and I'm not letting some outsider in—risking that cohesion, that integrity—now we're on the way up.'

'Well and truly up, from what I've heard.'

Rick shrugged, without complacency or false modesty. 'We've done well, commercially, yes. We've conquered the mass market, because that's what I set out do do. With a bit of cheek and a lot of graft, it's not so difficult.'

'Some people wouldn't find it so straightforward,' Vanessa observed.

'No, I realise that. But when I decide to accomplish something...' He shrugged again, expressively. 'So, there's plenty of money in it. If that's the main point, we've succeeded, which might be enough for most people. For most managers, particularly,' he added heavily. 'But for me . . . for us . . . well, in certain important respects, we're only just starting out.'

'What respects?'

'Artistically, creatively. I always intended to push against the boundaries of popular music, rather than stay contentedly within them, even more than we've done so far. And I will—any minute now! It's all going to happen! I've got some ideas, Vanessa, you'd better believe it!'

'Ideas?' She was intrigued to see such vigorous enthusiasm in action. It was a rare commodity, and an exciting one.

'Musical, and—what shall we say?—social. The things that could be achieved via this mass medium! The impact that could be made!'

'You see yourself as another Bob Geldof?'

'Not exactly. What he did was fantastic, but I meant more in the line of raising funds, and consiousnesses, through our own performances, not getting other artists to do it for us.'

'I see what you mean. Very commendable.'

'No need to sound so cynical about it, Vanessa. I'm not pretending there isn't plenty in it for us, too.'

'I'm not in the least cynical, just a bit . . .'

'Surprised? Yes, well, fair enough. You've got a lot to learn—about me.' With an abrupt, impatient movement, he clunked his empty cup down on the desk, then ran a hand through the thickness of his hair. 'Anyway, what the hell am I doing, telling you all this? This is supposed to be the big reconciliation scene, and here I am, regaling you with more facts and fancies than I've ever divulged to a press interviewer in my life!'

'You're telling me because I asked you,' Vanessa pointed out.

'So you did. Just making polite conversation?'

'Not at all!' she protested. 'I want to know. I'm interested.' The only surprising thing was, it was true.

'I could almost believe you.' He stared at her for a moment, then slid down from the desk and paced over to look out of the window at the rolling green acres. *His* acres, hard-won, well deserved, though twenty-four hours ago Vanessa would never have conceded such a thing.

'Why shouldn't I be interested? My own brother's mad about—about the whole pop scene. And apparently about Totem, along with the rest of it. Isn't it natural I should want to understand?' It was easier to be emphatic, faced with his back view. Her eyes were riveted to the spot where his fair hair lapped over his shirt collar. His hands were thrust into his pockets.

He swung round, catching her out. The blue eyes were sharp and shrewd. 'It may be natural, but I haven't gained the impression you've wasted a lot of sleep over it up to now, Vanessa. Seems to me you've dismissed the *whole pop scene*, as you call it, with one wave of your dainty classical hand. Squelched it under your fastidious classical foot.'

Vanessa cringed, but rose to the challenge. 'Mark's never really encouraged me to take an interest. It's something we argue about but never really follow through. I mean, he still quite likes some classical music—I think—he always used to

when he was little. But he never actually gets me
to sit down and *listen* to any of his sort of stuff...'

'And have you ever asked to?' Rick was there
before her. 'I mean, have you ever listened to *us*,
for instance?'

'No, but I do hear his records all the time.'

'Through walls and floors? Muffled? Resenting
every minute of it? Bristling with disapproval when
it clashes with Radio Three, or your own choice of
entertainment?' He was scathingly accurate. 'Oh,
I know the score, Vanessa, and this is just what I
wanted to talk to you about. This is why I dragged
you in here, instead of packing you off home.'

'You didn't drag me anywhere. I was only too
glad of the chance to draw breath before...'

'Be that as it may, this is the point. I want you
to hear this. I was brought up in a home where two
generations—two cultures—continually rubbed
each other up the wrong way, causing constant irritation and aggro for all concerned. It became
second nature. So, I know where you're at, Vanessa Davies: you don't just *prefer* classical music;
you've made a decision to reject any other. You
refuse to consider any other kind. It's an irrational
philosophy, totally uninformed, based on nothing
but sheer blind prejudice!'

'How can you say that?' Vanessa sat bolt upright
in her chair. Their eyes clashed. 'It's fine for
you...you obviously had all the opportunities! You
say there was this conflict of cultures in your home,
so you understand Mark, but from the way you
play—the amount you know—you must have had
a proper classical education! You must be a trained
musician, so you could have been...could be...'

'Could be what, Vanessa?' Now Rick came over to her, sitting in the other armchair, leaning forward. 'What could I be? Tell me?'

'Why waste it on all this, when...?'

He sighed, and Vanessa automatically braced herself for a parry. But instead of raising his temperature to match hers, he was in rigid control, steady and reflective. 'Waste, waste...yes, I've heard it all before! I know how your mind works, and it's boring! Petty! Insular! It would be sad enough from well meaning parents, with heads buried in the dark ages, but in someone with *your* sensitivity—intelligence—someone of *your* age...a bloody crime, that's what it is!'

He waited to see whether she would rise to the bait, but she was struck dumb—mainly by the precise echo of Mark's sentiments, embodied in Rick's words.

Palms down, he spread his two hands on his knees as he continued. 'I know you haven't had an easy time, and I appreciate your sacrifices. I do respect what you've done. Who wouldn't? I'm damn sure Mark does! It must have been tough for you, but is that a reason to grow middle-aged and narrow-minded before your time?'

Vanessa's mouth opened and closed, fishlike, foolish. There could be no possible reply to such cruel probings. Was it empty slander, adding insult to injury? Or did it carry a grain of truth? And either way, why should it concern him?

Perhaps in response to her silence, he leaned even nearer, and now his tone carried a new gentleness, tinged with sadness. 'Listen to me, Vanessa. I agreed to let Mark come up here, when Ron asked me, because I have a lot of sympathy for a discriminating youngster who's crazy about good rock music and wants to make it himself. And I know, better than anyone, the frustration that can cause: wondering how to develop the urge, or where to take it. It's a massive jungle, the whole business. How do you start?'

He paused, again to see if she would react, but she simply let him go on. All the time, he seemed to creep overwhelmingly closer, entering her private space.

'You're not wrong. I had all the breaks when it came to the full traditional education. Proper piano lessons from five years old, child prodigy in the making. I passed every Associated Board exam with distinction. I went to music college, straight from school, and studied organ, timpani, and conducting. I gained merits all round.' He reeled the major achievements off as if they were a shopping list. 'I enjoyed it well enough—but all the time I was straining at the leash, waiting for...'

'Did you say conducting?' Vanessa found a husky voice at last.

Rick was stopped in his tracks. 'I did. You know, the wielding of the baton? The directing of the orchestra? The full maestro bit? For your information, I was good at it—showed promise.'

'I'll bet.' *I'll bet you were! That's exactly how I pictured you!*

'Oh, yes, I could have made a career in it. They all said so.'

'What a loss to the world of music!' This bitterness was swelling up in Vanessa, but she pushed through it. 'So, what made you choose all this instead?'

He was watching her, so closely; his tone was so intense.

'No, that doesn't express it. I didn't choose *all this*; it chose me. When the crunch came, this was the way I felt called. This is what I feel I do best. Can't you relate to that?'

'I suppose, if reaching the most people—the biggest audiences—is what you're after...' Vanessa was twisting her hands in her lap, but she faced him. 'I don't expect your parents could—relate to it, could they?'

His eyes darkened. 'Too right, they couldn't! Eventually, when I was a grown man and well into my stride, they came to terms with it—after a fashion. Even *they* can see I might have something going for me in this sinful rock business, after all. Even *they* can't ignore the fact I've done pretty well out of it.'

'Wasn't that what you wanted, originally?' Vanessa had every sympathy for his parents.

'No, it wasn't. I dare say I set out to prove something—to them, and to myself—as a result of their attitude. I dare say I was driven much further in this direction than I might have been otherwise, without their opposition all along the line. That's the point I'm trying to make, Vanessa. Now maybe you see why it's relevant to you?'

'Oh, I see all right. I've seen, ever since you mentioned it.'

'Ten years ago, when I was about Mark's age, if my parents had thought I was planning any such future, they'd have flipped their combined lid. *The insecurity! The waste!* Not what they had in mind for their only son...their blue-eyed boy...'

'Hmmm.' Vanessa could envisage it all.

'They were so obstructive, you wouldn't believe! You'd have thought it was criminal tendencies, or drugs, I wanted to get into. I was reduced to slinking furtively off to a friend's house to play my own records. Blatant lying to go to pop concerts.'

'Mark and I haven't quite reached that stage,' Vanessa commented drily.

'No, maybe not. But I bet you don't allow him to actually make music in the house—not properly with others—do you?'

'No, I do draw the line at that. I don't stop him going to concerts, or playing his records. I don't stop him going to someone else's house and making all that noise...'

'See what I mean? *Making all that noise.* You won't give it house room, will you? You'd rather banish it from reality.'

'It's not as bad as that,' Vanessa insisted.

'And how does he finance these activities? Buy the discs, equipment, tickets? I can't imagine *you* subsidising any of it.'

'He has a weekend job at a record shop. He takes a pride in making his own way. And that's got nothing to do with my opinion of his musical tastes.' There was an equal pride—a defiance—in Vanessa's declaration. She might not approve Mark's choice of obsession, but she did appreciate his single-mindedness in maintaining it.

'This is such familiar territory! I had about six paper-rounds to finance mine. Mind you, I reckon that's quite a good thing.' Rick's gaze had wandered away, inwards; now it snapped back to Vanessa's. 'And what about the rest?'

'What rest? What do you mean?'

'I mean, I can see *Doorsteps* is thriving, but does it pay the household bills?'

For a moment she was alarmed and offended at the intrusion, but then she relaxed. This was an open, candid confrontation, and there was no point in becoming defensive now.

'My father—my parents were well insured, so they didn't leave us destitute. The house is paid up, and there was enough to invest for a reasonable income. You might say *Doorsteps* puts the butter on our bread, and some of the jam too, but it hasn't been making a profit very long.'

'Mankind cannot live by smorgasbord alone.' But Rick hadn't missed her dignity, or honesty. 'I imagine young Mark recognises your efforts on his behalf, all down the line, even if he doesn't say much.'

'Oh, yes, he does! He's marvellous, in most ways. We've always pulled together, ever since...because of what happened. We get on really well, much better than some sisters and brothers—we have to! We hardly ever argue. That's why I find it so hard to understand...'

Vanessa was drained from her own eruption of emotion. Expelling all this was like being forced to open creaky floodgates.

Rick leaned back, hands behind head. He seemed to be weighing each word, as if to make sure it was accurately chosen.

'Has it ever occurred to you, Vanessa, that Mark might be a bit short on rebellion? It's not quite natural at his age, such sweetness-and-light, is it? I mean, all teenagers have to have their kick against authority, even if the authority takes the form of

a much-loved sister, not even half a generation older
than he is?'

Vanessa sat back now, retreating into her own
chair. She followed him closely, but made no
comment. He waited to see if she would, and then
continued—slowly, deliberately.

'If it's important to most adolescents, keeping
an area of separate identity, it must be absolutely
crucial to Mark. He owes you real solidarity—and
he gives it. In his way he carries a very heavy
burden, Vanessa. He needs a foil, a relief from that.
So, what does he choose?' Rick paused again,
waiting and watching, and again she kept silent.
'Well, Big Sister's Thing is classical music, so of
course he chooses that! What could be more
natural, as a target for conflict?' He chuckled. 'I
understand it's traditional in the best-regulated
families, even if the parents don't go to the ex-
tremes mine went to. Surely you must have done
something like that yourself, Vanessa, when you
were fourteen? Fifteen?'

Was she ever fifteen? 'I never liked pop music
much,' she hedged.

'I think we've gathered that. I meant, you must
have had your own versions of self-discovery...
minor rebellion? In the years before you found
yourself having to turn into substitute parent, friend
and comrade, instead of big sister and grown-up
daughter?'

'Perhaps...I don't know...I can hardly
remember...'

'Think about it, that's all I'm saying. If you tried
to see Mark's obsession as something positive—
something that could be a lot worse... After all,'
he grinned, 'pop music—good rock music—has

impeccable roots. It's wholesome enough, it's universally accepted, and it's legal, harmless, non-addictive.'

She took his point; but the more sense he made, the more sceptical she sounded. 'If you say so.'

'And from what I hear, in Mark's case, the craze goes deep. He's got some genuine talent at the guitar, and at song-writing, according to Ron Scully.'

'First I've heard of it,' Vanessa muttered.

'You'd be the last to hear of it. Take my word, the more serious he is, the less likely he is to confide in you about it, especially if your attitude's been negative. He'll play you up—muck you about—use it as a point of friction.'

'Friction.' Vanessa repeated the word to herself, as her mind churned over Rick's bombardment of ideas. This was more like a session with a psychiatrist than the simple practical transaction she had been expecting when she'd left home this morning.

'You've got such spirit, Vanessa. I can tell you feel strongly about things. There's nothing wrong with that; so do I. That's why I wanted you to understand why *I* feel so strongly about this business with Mark and the work experience. It's a personal point with me. Can you see that?'

Suddenly he was on the edge of his chair, half crouching, leaning over—and seizing Vanessa's hands in his. The gesture was so unhesitating, it rendered her helpless. Like being swept, literally, off her two feet by a typhoon gust, and deposited, hanging upside down, from a high branch. Winded, disadvantaged, mentally and physically jolted.

He was still speaking, even as he did it. 'We're none of us totally unselfish, are we, Vanessa? In the end, it all revolves around each one of us: *our* emotions, *our* experiences. In the end, try as we might to act altruistically, it boils down to Number One. Isn't that right?'

With each sentence, he was drawing her towards him. His voice was pitched low, soft, yet vibrating with messages. She sensed them, rather than fully comprehending them. Her mind resisted, but her body was calling the tune. It glided sweetly into his force field, smoothly as a swan on a glassy lake.

'Isn't that right, Vanessa?' he was repeating, but the murmur was all but lost as the space between them diminished, and vanished—all on the subtle strength of that magnetic pull from his hands on hers. His face was acutely clear; then it was a blur, and her eyes closed, as their lips touched at last. Lightly, the merest brush; then lingeringly—clingingly—an experimental tasting, a long moment of mutual discovery, millions of miles beyond the power of words or ideas.

Vanessa was competent with words, and adept with ideas. But in this particular area of life she wasn't just rusty, she was thoroughly rustproofed. As a means of communication it had been sealed off for years. Five, to be exact. Now, along with those other floodgates, some even deeper ones opened. A torrent had been dammed up, and it was ripe to burst, and now it came surging through the barriers, swirling her away.

At first she wallowed in the new sensation, revelled in the warm powerful currents as they welled up. Then she was afraid, certain they would drown her. She fought free, leaped back, tugged her hands away; then opened her dark, dazed eyes to stare into his brilliant blue ones.

There was humour there, aimed at the reproach in hers. He was playing with her, and she grew instantly flustered and furious.

'I didn't mean . . . I'm sorry . . .'

'Why, Vanessa? *I'm* not.'

What was she mumbling about? Why should *she* be sorry? *He* was the one who had made the running in all this! And the happily married one, to boot. *She* was his passive target, his victim. Why *should* she be sorry?

But evidently such scruples were beyond him, and he hadn't finished with her yet. Now he was reaching over to slide one light fingertip along her cheek, tracing the curve of it down to her mouth.

'Well, you should be!' Vanessa retreated into the depths of her chair, folding her arms protectively across her chest.

'I might be—if I thought that was the closest I was ever going to get to you, Vanessa.' He was satirical, but also solemn, and the blend was bewildering. 'What's the big deal, anyway? We're both consenting adults, aren't we? You're not spoken for, are you?'

'No, but . . .'

'I thought not.' He nodded—smugly, she thought. 'Far too busy, aren't you—being parent, sibling and breadcutter rolled into one? So, where's the harm? Haven't you got to have some private life, too?' Catching her paranoid expression, he laughed aloud. 'You don't want to go believing everything you hear about my notorious profession, darling. Sure, we do have a tendency to be chased— I mean C-H-A-S-E-D. But—don't breathe a word

of this to my fans,' he whispered wickedly, 'some
of us are quite chaste. C-H-A-S-T-E,' he spelt out,
in case she had missed the point.

Vanessa stared down at her hands, neatly folded
in her lap, prim...chaste. 'I'm not your darling,'
she muttered.

'Forgive me—it was a lapse, the merest manner
of speaking; no profound significance intended. Or
perhaps it was a Freudian slip—a weak moment of
wishful thinking?'

This had gone far enough. Before Vanessa realised what she was doing, she was on her feet and
making for the door, fighting a nameless panic.

'I—I must go! I really must!'

But it was not a wise move. In a second, he was
standing in her path; then his hands were on her
shoulders, fingers unyielding on her upper arms,
imprinting themselves through the layers of clothing
to the skin beneath, raw and red-hot.

'I haven't quite done with you yet!'

She remained silent and still, in his grasp.

'There's one more thing I want to say to you, my
friend. Just five more minutes, OK?' His fingers
loosened, and she could have ducked free, but she
nodded. Letting her go, he sat down again, and she
did the same—tense, watchful.

'I'm a very private guy, Vanessa. Circumspect is
my middle name. I don't give many interviews, and
I don't get involved in rumour, gossip, or speculation. I keep my personal life personal. Hardly
anyone outside the group knows about this place,
for example, and I want to keep it that way.'

'*I* won't be telling anyone, if that's what you're
afraid of. But it's common knowledge in the village
already.'

'We can't expect to keep it quiet locally. Anyway, I want to be part of the community—give something to it, not just make use of it—so inevitably people are going to learn who we are. No, that isn't what I was getting at. It was about you.'

'Me?'

'I've told you things about me—formative experiences—that I rarely talk about to anyone, least of all an outsider.'

'I'm deeply honoured.'

He ignored her sarcasm. 'And you've opened up, too, about Mark—and your parents.'

She did not wince at the reference. 'It's all right, I've told you, I'm quite OK about that now.'

'I know. But there's something else, isn't there?'

'Is there?'

'We've neatly skirted around it, all this time. Haven't we?'

'Have we?' What was he getting at now?

'Your singing, Vanessa.'

'Ah!'

'That's right: *ah*! So, what's it all about?'

'There's no mystery. As I told Ellie, I used to sing a bit, that's all.' But Vanessa was deeply flushed, and hoarse.

'Look, lady, I'm no idiot, and I'm a fair judge of human nature. There's more to it than that, I know there is.' He gave her three seconds—four—five to find a reply, then he leaned nearer. She was so fraught, she only half registered his hand on her knee. 'You planned to train as a professional singer, didn't you? You'd have gone to college, wouldn't you? You'd set your heart on it as a career—hadn't you?'

Vanessa waited patiently for the room to reel and shimmer and quake, as the world always did when this acute pain was triggered off. But it stayed tolerably still. Furthermore, Rick's face did not dissolve into a tear-distorted image of itself.

Whatever extraordinary shifts were going on, this was a step in the right direction at least. She drew a long, faltering breath. She might not quite understand his game, but she refused to be beaten at it.

'As a matter of fact, yes, you're right. I'm a passable soprano, or could have been, if I'd had the training. Had the education—like you.'

Rick was in no way fooled by her blasé smile. 'You were on the point of going off to get precisely that training, weren't you? When the accident to your parents happened?'

This time she merely nodded. His hand was becoming warm and heavy on her knee. His body was tantalisingly close to hers, though scarcely touching.

'You had to give up the idea, didn't you, to stay and take care of Mark?'

'I didn't mind, really.' But her tone and expression betrayed her.

'No need to get defensive! This is pure sacrifice we're talking about—martyrdom, even—no cause for shame, surely?' He was homing in again, right on target. 'Vanessa, you *did* mind! You minded a lot, didn't you? And you've never stopped minding, have you?'

'There are other things more important in life than doing what you want.' It was a pious retort, and a futile one. 'Anyway, once Mark's through school, once he's decided what he wants to do next—university or what—well, then I'll be free to pick up where I left off.'

'Will you, Vanessa? Are you sure?'

'Why not?' But her mouth was dry and her throat tight.

'You know the answer to that as well as I do. Professional singers are made, not born. They need to start training young, like all musicians, if they're going to get anywhere in a competitive world. It may not be too late in a couple of years' time, but it won't be half so good as it would have been five years ago. Will it?'

'Perhaps not, but that won't stop me trying. If...'

'If you can get the confidence together. If you can pass the tests and auditions. If you can afford it. If.'

Vanessa could only shake her head. He was only too appallingly right, on all counts. She rarely let herself think about this any more, but it was always there, a cruel, staccato counterpoint to the fluent phrasing of her daily life.

'You see? I do understand.' He was almost tender. She stared down—away—anywhere, because nothing cut deeper into her composure than concern. 'You were thwarted in your ambition...'

'Not thwarted!' The word galvanised her into speech. 'I *chose* to stay here! It wasn't Mark's fault! He needed me!'

'Nevertheless, you were thwarted, whether you chose or not. Mark was only a child, and yes, he needed you. Unless you moved to somewhere nearer where you wanted to study, you had to stay here.'

'I already had a place at the Royal Academy in London.' This was the most painful part, but she spat it out. 'Not a chance of us both moving there!

Mark was just starting at the school here. All his friends were here. All our roots. It's been our home all his life, and most of mine. The house...I couldn't face the upheaval...going to college and looking after him at the same time...'

'So, don't deny you were thwarted. And thwarted people grow to be twisted inside, with resentment and bitterness, eventually—maybe without realising it themselves. You're already going in that direction, Vanessa. Isn't that what all this performance is about? All this rage about Mark—his music—and me and my dual culture, which you can't stomach? My opportunities wasted, and all that stuff?'

'I'm *not* bitter! I'm *not* twisted inside!'

'Not yet, perhaps. On the outside, you're anything but, and I don't know the inside of you, yet.' That *yet* sliced through her, setting up a whole series of complex ripples of its own. 'But you will be, if you go on holding it all in. One day you'll wake up and find you're a crabby old lady, who's never forgiven herself for that piece of self-denial all those years ago. Noble, though it was—admirable— loving—unselfish. Not only not forgiven yourself, but not forgiven Mark either, or your parents, or the world in general.'

He was merciless. Vanessa felt she was being physically pulped. 'But Mark never even *knew* about it—not really! And my parents didn't *choose* to...to...'

It was a pathetic attempt at an argument, and now her voice did crack and quaver. Even as she rose unsteadily to her feet, on another blind instinct to flee, he was ready to catch her. Then he was holding her hard against his warm, solid frame.

Unconsciously her hands came up to clutch at his chest—the front of his shirt. Her head was bent forward: the pony-tail slipped out of its moorings, the curtain of dark hair falling, masking her face so that all he saw was the top of the shining head.

'All the same, I reckon there's part of you needs to forgive them for what happened, and get this block out of your system. Otherwise you're going to suffer, and so is Mark.'

'What can I do? Rick, what can I do?'

He had to stoop to catch the question. Her eyes were dry, but the words trembled on tiny, sighing sobs. Hearing them, he became supremely firm and gentle.

Instead of answering, he posed a question of his own. 'What were you going to study at the Academy? Along with the singing? You need another subject—a subsidiary—don't you?'

'Composition... music theory... history of music... piano. Any of those, I didn't know. I wasn't sure then. Singing was always the main thing. I wanted to do it... so much...'

'What sort of singing, Vanessa?'

'Anything! Recitals, opera, anything.'

'Solo?'

'Of course, if I ever got good enough. They all thought I could be... I intended to be.'

'You were all set to be a *diva*? A proper little *prima donna*?'

He was teasing. Anxiously, she studied his face. He had built this new kind of instant trust, and if he shattered it now...

But his expression was calm—reassuring. 'It's obvious what you ought to be doing, I'd have thought,' he said.

'Is it?'

'Practice, of course. You should be keeping that larynx limbered up, those tonsils in trim, ready for when they're needed.'

'Oh yes? How?' Now she frowned. It was all very well, Rick Seymour pontificating from his ivory tower—the top of his Totem Pole—with all the advantages, years of fulfilled ambition behind him and everything going for him. 'I warble in the bath, if that's what you're about to suggest. I sing along with Maria Callas, in Verdi and Wagner, in the privacy of my sitting-room. Then there's Kiri te Kanawa,' she declared. 'One of my top three. She and I have a rich fantasy life together. You should hear our *Marriage of Figaro,* and my *Madame Butterfly...'*

'No need to get clever.' Rick smiled, but never released his hold on her. 'That wasn't quite what I had in mind.'

'So what was?'

'It's obvious, isn't it? What about local performances? Amateur operatics? Recitals? I've noticed there's a lot of it round here. You don't have to look far, and you don't have to be an expert.'

'The church choir, you mean? The Compton Choral Society? Pantomime? Gilbert and Sullivan?'

Now he held her at arm's length, the blue eyes sharp on her. 'Not being the tiniest bit élitist again here, are we? Cutting off our vocal cords to spite our face? Do I detect a hint of cultural bigotry?'

'It's not that! It's *any* public singing—anywhere! I just...'

'I think you catch my drift, Vanessa. Martyrdom—resentment. It feeds on itself, so before you know where you are, you've grown all self-righteous, full of excuses, and you don't *do* anything. I know—I've been there, and I'm telling you, the secret is action—active participation. Get out there and throw your weight about a bit. Don't lurk in the background, gnashing your pretty teeth.' He paused to let all this sink in. 'Lots of singing, in public, as often and as loudly as possible. That's what this doctor prescribes for you, Vanessa Davies.'

'I couldn't...I can't...' She stared at him through wide, startled eyes.

Before he could push her any further, there was a knock at the door. Vanessa jumped back, stung. Rick sauntered over to open it, and collided with Ellie, who rushed in, all smiles as usual.

'Hey, you two—finished your confab? Feeling better, Vanessa? Thought I'd just tell you, they've all gone back up to the studios, so it's safe to come out now. There's a few of your pasties left over, and they've gone down a treat. Yummy, they were—everyone said so. You've got yourself some regular customers here. *Doorsteps* won't know what's hit it.'

'Good. Thanks.' Vanessa managed to smile back.

'You could be right there, Ellie.' Rick was smiling too. 'I don't think Doorsteps knows what's hit her. But I'm sure she's feeling better, aren't you, Vanessa?'

Ellie eyed him. 'What have you been doing to her, Rick? I know that look.' She turned to Vanessa. 'Has he been bullying you again?'

'No, no, nothing like that. I'm fine. The coffee and biscuits were lovely, just what I needed. Thanks, Ellie. Now I must...'

'Have a pasty or two, before you leave? You must be famished!'

'No, I'm not, really. I'll just get off home. I'm rather tired, and Mark might phone and wonder where I am all this time.'

'Of course. We've kept you here far too long, as it is. Funny, isn't it, the way things work out? Bet you didn't think you'd be spending half the day up here?'

'Yes, I mean no, I didn't. It's certainly—strange.'

'Certainly is.' Rick's contributions were concise and cryptic.

Ellie escorted Vanessa through a kitchen which had apparently been devastated by a hurricane. 'Come up and watch us record any time—oh no, I forgot, you're not really...'

'I'm afraid I haven't quite converted Vanessa, but I might just have persuaded her to reconsider about Mark.' Rick stood at the back door now, leaning on the frame, nonchalant.

'Mark?' Half-way to her car, she hesitated. 'I don't know...'

'Think it over,' Rick suggested.

'Yeah, do that! Don't let him pressurise you! He's a tyrant, this man!' Ellie rested a hand affectionately on his shoulder. Vanessa stared at them both, then opened her car door.

'I'll have another word with Mark about it.' That was a major concession. She knew it, and so did Rick.

She revved the engine, squealed the tyres in a frenetic three-point turn, and made off down the drive without glancing back.

CHAPTER SIX

'VANESSA, you've got to be having me on!'

Carol, matronly young mother, actually bounced on her chair. Round eyes fixed on Vanessa; intrigue packed into every stitch of her pretty plump frame.

'All true, I swear.'

'The cheek! You go up there to deliver a few snacks, and end up receiving a lecture on relative cultural values! So, what happened?'

'How do you mean, happened?'

'Well, did you finally agree to let Mark go up there, or what?'

'Not exactly. I said I'd think about it and I'm still thinking.' Vanessa gave her wet hair a vigorous rub, then wrapped the towel round it, turban style.

'And?'

'And what?'

'Nothing else?'

'What did you expect?' Vanessa hedged. 'I said goodbye, and went.'

'Oh.' Carol looked vaguely disappointed. 'With the money, of course?'

Vanessa's smile grew slightly stiff. 'Well, as a matter of fact...'

'You mean, after all that, you never even *got* the money?'

'Somehow, it slipped my mind. It was all so...unexpected...'

'Not like you, Nessa. Not like you at all.' But Carol was far more curious than reproachful. 'Not to worry, we can send them a bill, as usual. You must have been annoyed with yourself, though.'

'I was, when I realised.' Extremely annoyed.

'I don't know whether I pity you or envy you,' Carol mused. 'I mean, to be cornered like that—and by Rick Seymour, of all people...'

'I should stick with the pity.' *Cornered*. That was one word for it.

'And as for him being married to Ellie Dale! They've certainly kept it quiet! I've noticed that she wears a ring, but she wears a lot of rings—it's part of her style, and I never imagined...wait till I tell the Young Wives Group about this!'

'No, Carol!' Vanessa almost spilled her coffee as she jerked upright.

'No what?'

'You're not to tell them, or anyone, about all this. Please! It's between you and me, in strict confidence. Rick would be furious if...'

'Oh, so it's *Rick* now, is it?'

'You can hardly expect me to call him *Mr Seymour*, after we've...

'You've what?' Carol was a trusting person, not a cynic, but now she was staring at Vanessa in open suspicion.

'Conducted an informal transaction, and a—fairly personal conversation.' Inadequate phrases for what had really taken place—not even the tip of the iceberg—but more than enough for Carol's eager ears.

But Carol was nodding, satisfied. 'I can see he wouldn't be the kind of man to deal in surnames and all that official stuff. I can imagine him wanting to know *your* first name too, if he was so interested?'

'He wasn't interested!' Vanessa's tone sharpened, scolding Carol just as she'd been busily scolding herself these past two days. 'He was piqued, that's all. I caused a minor case of punctured male pride. He's not used to being rejected, he's used to being flattered and wooed by sycophantic admirers. It'll do him good to know the sun doesn't shine out of...'

After a quick glance, Carol had already decided to change tack. 'It'll be good for trade, anyway. You've done us a favour there, I bet. I can see it now, painted on the van: *By Appointment to Totem*. If they liked our pasties as much as all that, they'll be back for more.'

'So Ellie implied.'

'Is she as nice as she seems? I always think she looks sweet.'

'She's lovely.' Vanessa had no hesitation in confirming that. 'I wish I'd known she was their singer, though. Might have saved me a few embarrassing moments.'

'I thought everyone knew what Totem looks like. Even you.'

'Evidently you were right. Apart from me, that is.'

'Never mind.' Carol leaned back contentedly as she sipped her coffee. 'You know now, and you'll know next time.'

'What next time?'

But Carol ignored the muttered comment, aimed into Vanessa's coffee mug rather than at anyone in particular. She stretched, gazing round Vanessa's tidy, bright kitchen. 'Hey, isn't this the life? I could do with a bit more of this! A whole Tuesday morning with no Johnny, and no orders for *Door-*

steps! I know I shouldn't say it, about either of them, but it's wonderful to have such an outbreak of peace!'

'If anyone deserves a break, it's you. You've had a difficult time lately. It's good to see you relaxing, and to have you round here for a change, instead of...'

'I know, I know. Trying to conduct a civilised conversation in my cluttered domain, with Johnny underfoot, and all the rest of it.'

Vanessa was glad of any opportunity to shift the focus off herself and on to her friend. It had been so tempting to share the burden of that crazy visit to the manor; but when it came to the point, what could she really give away? Not even edited highlights—more like tactfully selected lowlights, if everyone's honour was to be preserved.

'Well, it's good to know things are looking brighter on the home front,' she said. 'I'm so glad Ken finally got the problem off his chest. And that Johnny's better enough to go and play with Dean.'

'Equal relief all round,' Carol agreed, smiling across at her. 'And thanks for being here and listening, too. That was Ken's trouble: bottling it all up. It's so important to keep in touch, talk things over! Don't ever keep your worries to yourself, Nessa. I'm always here. It may not solve anything, but it does seem to make things clearer.'

'Thanks. I'll bear it in mind.'

'Right.' Carol was glancing at the clock, jumping to her feet. 'Reality calls! It's twelve, and I promised to pick the young thug up from Val's before lunch. With some regret, I must resume my maternal duties. It's been so refreshing, Vanessa.'

'I'm not doing you any favours. I've enjoyed it too. Come again.'

'Subject to the demands of *Doorsteps*, young Master John, *et al.*, I most certainly will.' Carol was locating her handbag and jacket.

Vanessa came to the front door with her. 'You don't ever regret your involvement with *Doorsteps*, do you, Carol?'

'Good lord, no! It's a lifeline—I love it. And the extra money comes in handy—could be handier, if things shape up the way they're looking at the moment...'

'That's OK then. Don't ever hesitate to say if it gets too much.'

'I won't, I promise. Now I'll have to dash.'

Carol was half-way down the path when an engine's roar caused Vanessa to glance up sharply. A motorcycle was rounding the corner. Not such an uncommon sight around here: several of the local youths strutted on two wheels. But these tended to be small and high-pitched, especially in comparison to this one now throbbing along the road, clearly packing a considerable punch.

The rider, entire face helmeted and visored, whole body encased in black leather, could have been any man on earth. In fact, he could have been a creature from any planet at all: Vanessa often thought they resembled astronauts or extra-terrestrial beings, rather than ordinary everyday humans, these dashing daredevils who actually chose to travel this way. It could have been Kerry's Charlie, except that this one appeared less scruffy, altogether better equipped. Probably it was some fellow fanatic of his, on the way out there. Mark would have recognised the type and make of machine at once. Va-

nessa tried to spot it, so that she could tell him when
he got home. Not easy, the speed it was going,
but...

But he was slowing down as he approached her
row of cottages. He seemed to be reading the
numbers. Slower—still slower. If he lost any more
speed, he'd surely topple over! Carol had stopped,
and was hovering near the gate. Something about
the sight of him—the unexpected arrival of this
modern centaur with the sleek torso and shoulders
of a man, welded to that potent lump of metal and
movement beneath—something gripped the attention of both women, so that they forgot themselves and each other.

The number of Vanessa's house was clearly em-
blazoned on her wrought-iron gate. The man noted
it, nodded, and brought his bike to a smooth halt.
Then there was the cutting out of that rich engine,
followed by an equally dense silence.

He swung his leg over the saddle, propped the
heavy machine up on its stand, sauntered round to
the pavement—and stood surveying his female re-
ception committee. Carol at the gate, Vanessa at
the door, both staring unashamedly at him. Then
the black-gloved hands came up to unfasten and
lift the massive globe of the helmet. Out of the im-
personal white casing—the ultimate disguise—
emerged a male head. Sharp, clean features; short,
tousled blond hair. The face smiled; not just the
long mouth, the vivid blue eyes as well.

As if mirroring his gesture, Vanessa's hands were
reaching up to adjust the towel round her head.
The moment of self-consciousness was more than
enough to compensate for the fact that the rest of
her body stayed motionless in the doorway.

So, Rick Seymour had tracked her down on her own patch? How? Or more pertinently, why?

If Vanessa was puzzled, Carol was downright enthralled, stepping back as Rick studied her, before transferring his stare to Vanessa. Then, abruptly, he vaulted over the low brick wall, landing lightly on the small front lawn.

He halted a couple of yards from Vanessa, standing with heavy boots planted firmly apart, one hand on hip, the other arm crooked around his helmet. His zipped leather jacket and jeans were close-tailored and supple. He peeled off the black gloves and thrust them in his pocket.

'There's no need to look so aghast,' he finally declared. 'I'm not a marauder, and I'm not an apparition. Nor am I a prisoner, up at the manor.' He indicated one black-clad ankle. 'No ball-and-chain. I'm free to come and go—within reason.'

'Incognito.' Vanessa nodded towards the motorcycle.

'There's no other way, in my situation.' He was resentful but resigned. 'I've tried everything else. In the early days we had the full megastar-mobile, the flash limo with the reflecting windows. That just attracted more attention than ever.'

'What a surprise!' Vanessa remarked.

'It was bad enough in London, but in a place this size it would be a disaster. I'd never escape beyond the gates.'

'My heart bleeds for you,' observed Vanessa. Meanwhile, Carol remained dumbstruck—trying, unsuccessfully, to prevent herself from gawping.

Rick was impervious to Vanessa's sarcasm or Carol's curiosity. 'After that I took to the roads in an ancient banger. For a while, it worked. No one recognised me—until the press got wind of it, I never knew how. Had to change my registration three times, and my car model twice. In the end I got fed up with that, too.'

'Well, you would,' Vanessa contributed.

'*Then* I hit on this notion of two wheels. I kept it dark, so no one was actually watching out for me aboard the thing. And with all the clobber on, even my own mother wouldn't pick me out. Anonymity at last!' And he smiled broadly at both of them.

'We won't tell, will we, Carol?'

'I'd be grateful. I don't mind local people getting to know; they're bound to. I'd rather it didn't become public knowledge, though.'

'We can't promise.' Vanessa became exaggeratedly rural. 'You knows what we country folk be like. Spreading tittle-tattle...'

'Terrible.' Carol giggled, finding her voice at last. 'But not to worry, Mr Seymour, your secret be safe with us.'

'I'm much obliged to you, ladies.' Rick bowed solemnly, but his eyes glinted. 'And the name is Rick,' he informed Carol.

She giggled again and blushed to the roots. 'I know.'

'I dropped by to see Vanessa. We have a small piece of unfinished business, I believe.'

'Have we?' Vanessa was sharp.

'I should say so.' Rick smiled enigmatically, then reached in his top pocket and waved a cheque book in her direction.

'Oh, yes, that. I remembered, as soon as I got home. I was about to send you the bill.'

'Then I've saved you the trouble.'

'There was no need,' Vanessa protested.

'Perhaps not. But as it happens, there was something else I wanted to see you about.'

It was said lightly, yet significantly. Vanessa glanced at him, then at Carol. Eventually, with clear reluctance, she said, 'Well, you'd better come in for a few minutes, then.'

Carol coughed. 'I'll have to be getting off, Vanessa.'

'Oh, Carol, I'm sorry!' Vanessa was flustered. 'Rick, this is my friend and colleague, Carol Lacey. She's responsible for the fillings in your snacks on Sunday, and the most accomplished cook in our...'

'Nonsense!' Carol was turning puce, as Rick strode towards her, one hand outstretched.

'Pleasure to meet you, Mrs Lacey! Any friend of Vanessa's and all that—especially if she's a part of *Doorsteps* as well! You're rated Number One at the manor. They're still drooling over those pasties. That's another reason I'm here: to place a permanent order.'

'I'm glad you liked them. And please call me Carol.'

Carol's hand still tingled from the firm grasp of his—but she was equally preoccupied, controlling a burst of irritation at his cool "Mrs". Of course he'd noticed such minor domestic details, being a married man himself, but it was peculiarly galling even so. 'I really must be going,' she announced with dignity. 'I have to collect John. My son,' she explained to Rick.

'Oh yes?' He was evidently fascinated. 'How old is he?'

'Only three.'

'Not reached the problem age yet, eh, Vanessa?' His smile grew more confusingly charming than ever. 'Glad to have met you, then—Carol.'

'Oh—er—yes. You too, I mean, me too.' Carol turned to Vanessa. 'See you soon. Thanks for the coffee. And take care!'

'And you, Carol!' Vanessa called. She started waving, but Carol was already a back view, purposefully receding down the road.

Vanessa hesitated, one hand on each side of her front doorframe, as if guarding her premises. Then she caught Rick's eye.

He was waiting patiently, thumbs hooked into belt, expression carefully neutral. Now he grinned, cocked his head and arched one fair eyebrow.

Vanessa shook her head, as if someone had asked her a question. Then she moved aside, leaving her threshold clear for him to come in. He passed close to her, and stopped in the hall, looking round.

'Great place, Vanessa. Peaceful atmosphere. Homely.'

'Untidy, you mean! This is my first free day for ages. I was about to have a good clear-up. I'd just washed my hair when Carol...'

'No need to apologise. It's me who ought to be doing that. I won't keep you long. I told them I'd be back soon.'

'I'm not apologising, just explaining.'

'Hey, you're all on edge.' He laid a hand on her shoulder, which did nothing to dispel the tension. 'Don't get all churned up! I've only come to settle my debts—remember?'

'Hmmm.' *And what else?* 'Well, I'll fetch a pen and my accounts file.' She twisted away, out of his reach. He was gazing round again.

'Yes, I really like the feel of this. It's all—very you, somehow.'

'We like it.' She shrugged.

'Of course you do: it's your home. It's a long time since I lived in a proper home.' She glanced at him, responding to something new in his tone: a wistfulness.

'Mind you,' he went on, 'the manor's a considerable improvement on some of the places I've lived in. Sordid bedsits, soulless apartments, the endless succession of interchangeable hotel rooms. Of course, that was the main reason we decided to buy it.'

He swung round, catching Vanessa out as she studied him with a new interest. Impatient at his own self-pity, he smiled again. 'Still, you know what they say: home is where the heart is. What the hell if it happens to be a castle or a caravan, as long as the company's right?'

'That's what they say.' Vanessa tensed again, but then—quite suddenly—she relaxed. 'For goodness' sake, put that helmet down and come in here!' She led the way into her sitting-room. 'Make yourself comfortable. Coffee? Sandwich? I was just thinking of...'

'No, thanks, Vanessa. I appreciate the invitation, but I said I'd be back. We've got this new housekeeper who started this week, and looks set to rule the kitchen with a spatula of iron. Plain English cooking, a bit stodgy and meaty for some of our number, but we can't complain. She's really on the ball, and there's no way I can keep every aspect of that great place under control—not if I'm going to supervise the conversion, as well as all the rehearsing, recording, booking...'

'Delegating a tiny slice of all that responsibility?' It was Vanessa's turn to be quizzical.

'Just the food. Nothing else.'

She smiled, soothingly. 'Sounds a good idea to me.'

'That's what Ellie said. But this lady's only coming on weekdays, so that's why we need to place a regular order with you—stock the freezer, then we'll always know we're OK after gigs, and at weekends.'

'I see.' Vanessa became brisk. 'Fine. Well, sit down, and please excuse me a minute, while I fetch my order book.'

'I'll talk among myself, don't worry.'

But Vanessa was already out of the room, and on the way to her study.

CHAPTER SEVEN

WHEN Vanessa returned, five minutes later, Rick had taken her at her word and made himself comfortable. He was ensconced in her largest armchair, serenely absorbed in a magazine. His bomber jacket was slung carelessly over the back of the sofa. Underneath it, he was wearing a brushed cotton shirt in bold checks of navy and dark grey.

For several seconds, they stared at one another, before dissolving into mutual laughter. It just happened that Vanessa had discarded her own sweater—and tucked into the trim waist of her slim black cords was a soft cotton shirt, almost identically checked in shades of grey and deep blue. She had also stopped to de-turban herself and comb out her hair, which now fell loose around her shoulders, damply dark, cleanly shining.

'Clothes, the great leveller of our era.' Vanessa sat in the next chair, pulled up a small table and bustled with her files.

Rick was watching her. 'But does it mean a meeting of minds? True kindred spirits, beneath the exterior uniform?'

'I wouldn't like to say.' She was still shuffling her papers.

'It's amazing how universal some styles are,' Rick reflected. 'Across generations, genders, classes, nationalities...'

'Unless you happen to be a real individualist, like Ellie.' Vanessa met his eye now, defiantly.

'Ah, Ellie!' Rick's expression softened. 'She has a style all her own! Individualist is the right word for our Ellie!'

Before Vanessa could reply, or even wonder why she'd felt such an urge to mention Ellie, he was leaning nearer, animated. 'Mind you, the strongest personalities might not need reinforcing through outward image. Had you thought of that? Anyway, it's part of Ellie's job. The public expects it, and she loves it. I've never bothered with all that—on stage or off. They have to accept me as I really am.'

'And obviously they do.' Vanessa was helplessly comparing Ellie—all that glowing panache—with her own neat simplicity. It was like a mockery, hanging in the air between them. 'Now, about this account . . .'

'To business.' Rick's cheque book appeared again, along with a smart gold pen. He unscrewed the top and sat poised to write. 'OK, so what's the damage? Tell me the worst.'

Vanessa passed him the bill. He perused it, and whistled. 'Seems remarkably reasonable! How the hell does *Doorsteps* make any profit at all? What you need is an expert manager. You're being exploited!'

'Not at all! It's a deliberate policy, keeping prices down so that we . . .' Then Vanessa subsided, realising he was teasing. She watched in silence as he wrote the cheque, signed it with a flourish and tore it out.

'Anyone would think I was advocating a transfer of total control! Now who's hanging on to every shred of responsibility?' But Vanessa was wise to him, and only made a face, so he grinned and started searching his pockets again. 'Now, where did I put that list we scribbled this morning—the regular order we want to put in—I'm sure I had it here somewhere...'

He half rose so that he could search in his trouser pockets. The bike leathers were certainly tight. Vanessa engrossed herself in staring at the cheque. Eventually he found the list and passed it over.

She looked up, taking it. 'Thanks.' The piece of paper was creased, and still warm from its sojourn in his back pocket. She studied it, but took in very little. Some lines of writing in a straight, strong, angular hand.

'Only slightly crumpled,' he said. 'Sorry about that. It's the bike—I can never carry anything properly.'

'It's fine. I'll check with my colleagues, and get back to you.'

'How many of you are there, besides you and Carol?'

'One other—our driver, Kerry.'

'The un-brawny chauffeuse?'

'That's right. She does some cooking, but mainly she's our equipment manager, and manic mechanic. She's really good with the van: the only problem is, she lives way out of the village and she doesn't have any other transport, so when something goes wrong with Gertrude I have to take over.'

Rick blinked. 'Gertrude?'

'The van.'

'Of course, I should have guessed. Who else would it be? So, we owe our encounter on Sunday to Kerry—and Gertrude.'

'Indirectly, yes.' Vanessa cleared her throat, and barged on. Anything to deflect that subject; anything to dispel this awareness that crept up around and between them, like an insistent cloud. 'Actually, Kerry's boyfriend would be interested in your bike. He's crazy about them. He's got three, and he's for ever tinkering with them. None of them are like yours, though. What make is it? I must tell Mark. He's pretty keen on them as well.'

'In common with many sixteen-year-old boys—like pop music.' Rick's comment was dead-pan. 'Well, you can tell Mark it's a Moto-Guzzi, and he's welcome to come and inspect it any time.'

The implication hit home, and Vanessa looked away, colouring. But Rick did not follow it up. 'Carol seems quite a character. What about her husband, is he a bike freak, too?'

'No, he's into electronics. He works with computers—programming and all that. I don't understand any of it, but I gather he's brilliant, and loves it, except...'

'Except what?' Noting Vanessa's frown, Rick sat upright.

'They've just had a bit of bad news. Carol was saying, only this morning...' Vanessa broke off. 'Why am I telling *you* this?'

Rick smiled. 'Because I'm asking you?'

Vanessa had to return the smile. She hesitated—and decided to continue. After all, Carol had only asked her not to tell too many people. 'He's being laid off, because his firm's—what was the word?—streamlining. I dare say he'll find another job, but it might mean a move. I hope not, and so do they. They like it here, and it would be a disaster for *Doorsteps* if we lost Carol, so...'

'Now, that's what I *call* a waste!' Rick seemed angry. 'Redundancy, the scourge of our times! Still, he should be in demand, this—what did you say his name was?'

'I didn't. It's Ken.'

'Well, he should be OK. Microchip Man, the new master race.'

After a slightly tense pause, they both spoke at once.

'Was there...?' began Vanessa.

'Before I go...' Rick grinned, then insisted 'after you,' with satirical courtesy.

Vanessa drew in a long breath. 'I was only wondering what else you wanted to say to me. If it was about Mark, I'm still—I haven't...'

'It wasn't about Mark, it was about you. I have a proposition, Vanessa.'

'Oh?' She waited for an explanation, but he sat back, folding his arms. 'What—what about me?' she murmured, at last.

'You remember what I was saying, about singing? My prescription for your state of—how shall I put it?—suspended animation? Getting out there, doing something positive, not letting it fester?'

'Yes.' How could she forget?

'Well, someone up there must have agreed with me, because today I bring divine backing. A special request, from the vicar.'

'The *vicar*?'

'Absolutely. The Rev Harte, in person. Did you know he's organising a public performance of *The Messiah* in the autumn? Fund-raising for the church? They've got dry rot in the tower, frayed bellropes, or was it bats in the belfry?'

'I hadn't heard,' Vanessa replied stiffly.

'He rang on Sunday night, and told me. He's hoping to recruit some local talent. He wondered if I might consider playing the organ for the gig.'

'And are you considering it?'

'You bet! More than considering it—I'm doing it. I didn't need asking twice. I dig Handel, especially *The Messiah*. It's like a great concept album, with chart-toppers in every track! And wasn't I saying to you on Sunday, we want to contribute to this community, not just take from it?'

'You were saying that, yes. So what? Why are you telling me all this?'

'Simple, isn't it, Vanessa? He wants singers, so I thought of you at once. I asked him, but he said he's given up trying to get you to join in such events, because you always refuse.'

'You had no right!' Vanessa was deeply flushed, fingers twisting in her lap as fear and fury writhed in her head.

'Good grief, woman, there's no need to throw a fit! I haven't committed you...I've merely...'

'You've merely taken it upon yourself to meddle in my affairs, when you know nothing about me, or them, or...'

'I may not have known you long, Vanessa,' he interrupted, quietly, 'but I believe I've learned a lot about you in that short time. From what you've told me—freely,' he pointed out.

'All the same, you might have consulted me first!'

'Listen, it came up, that's all. It's no big deal. I was interested to hear he'd tried—and others have tried—to get you out of your exile...your shell, whatever. Tried, and failed.'

'And you thought *you* might succeed?' In her agitation, she was sneering. 'I told you, I've got my reasons. I can't, that's all!'

Rick stared at her a moment; then all at once he was out of his chair and kneeling beside hers. His sudden closeness set up a jangle of contradictions: soothing, yet suffocating, healing, yet exacerbating this swelling wave of panic.

'Now listen to me. I'm sorry if this hurts you, but I've been giving it a lot of thought, and it seems to me you need encouraging.'

'You mean, *you* don't like being—thwarted, once you've...'

But he simply cut through her bitterness, taking hold of her hands, which still trembled and twisted together. 'I'm not denying there's an element of personal challenge for me, Vanessa. But I'm not doing this for my sake, I'm doing it for yours. People closest to you may not see what you need, but I do. After all, I'm objective, I'm not involved, so I've consigned myself the job. Hate me, if you must: I can take it!'

'Don't flatter yourself!' Vanessa glowered at their linked hands. Even the comfort of hating the man was hollow, when he was calmly inviting her to do just that. 'I don't care one way or the other; about you, I mean. I just don't see why you're bothering.'

'The idea of Mark had already grabbed me, before I'd met you. Now you, and your hang-ups, intrigue me even more, as a student of human nature. You can wriggle and squirm as much as you like——' his grip on her hands tightened, '—but I'm not letting go till we've sorted this thing out.'

'And if I don't care to be—sorted out?'

'Tough! I shall gaze into your smouldering eyes, admire your glowing cheeks, and tell you you're gorgeous when you're angry. Then you can get even angrier and accuse me of being the worst male chauvinist swine.'

He was impossible. It was like trying to do battle against an eel with a wry sense of humour.

'So—you're playing the organ, at this concert?'

'That's right—and that's not all. Ellie's taking part too, the contralto lead. And some of the others might...'

'*Ellie?*' Vanessa's mouth fell open. 'In *The Messiah*?'

'Why not?' His eyes narrowed. 'Watch it, Vanessa! Your preconceptions are showing again!'

'But—Ellie's not that sort of singer—is she?'

'What *sort* would that be?' His fingers were so tight on hers, the nails must be cutting into her skin. His tone had hardened at the same time.

But Vanessa rose valiantly to her own defence. 'You know what I mean, Rick! The sort of singer that sings in oratorio, that's all.'

'Ellie hasn't been classically trained, but she has a fine natural alto voice, and she can read a score. She's done *The Messiah* before. She loves all kinds of music—just as I do. The Reverend was delighted: nothing fuddy-duddy about him. It'll be great publicity, he reckons, and should pack 'em in, when the performance comes. I believe "bums on pews" was the expression he used: rather good, I thought.'

'It'll pack them in, all right.' Vanessa was incredulous.

'What they need now is a competent soprano. Nothing fancy, but better than anyone in the church choir. A reliable, tuneful voice. Of course, you might not be up to learning such a major part?'

'As it happens, I know most of it.' She rose instantly to the bait.

'How about it, then?'

'I can't, Rick. I'm not...'

'Then it's high time you could.'

'I couldn't, Rick.' Her plea was a tiny cry of defeat, half-lost on an indrawn breath. He was kneeling close beside her, his face level with hers. His hands drew her towards him again; and again she mindlessly obeyed the summons. Again that eclipsing of will, that totality of submission.

His eyes were devastatingly lucid, and so near, filling her vision. Then they blurred, too close for clarity. His voice was a presence which she felt rather than heard—a warmth fanning her skin, the sense of his words piercing direct through the cells and into her brain, instead of through her ears; bypassing thought.

'Active participation, Vanessa. Personal catharsis. Let it all hang out, as dear Ellie might advise.'

Ellie? Vanessa jerked back, on a last logical impulse. But it was too late for scruples now: his, or hers. He had captured her; he was calling the tune.

This time, the tasting, his lips on hers, was brief and impatient. This time his mouth quickly grew hot, demanding—a living, scorching flame—and Vanessa had no choice but to melt into it. To dissolve, diffuse against it, merge with it, until no boundaries or inhibitions were left intact. She was all liquid feeling, no more solid thinking; moving beyond her own control, and into his.

His hands abandoned hers, to creep up her arms to her shoulders, then to slide up her neck, and frame her face—one on either side of her head, fingers tangled in glossy dark hair. Now he gathered her up, so that she slipped effortlessly from her chair to the floor, clasped hard against him. She was weak—weightless—breathless. His body supported hers, even as it dominated; even as his hands were bending her head back, back, so that he could take more and yet more of the sweetness she yielded.

The kiss went on a long, long time, until finally—reluctantly, lingeringly—Rick was the one to draw away.

The sharp gaze explored Vanessa's transfigured face—the parted, glistening lips, the drugged, shadowed eyelids; then the bruised brown depths of the eyes that flickered half-open, overflowing with pleasure and pain.

Seeing him, she came to her senses at last. And not before time. Reality was a sledgehammer, assaulting her from behind. His fingers slid from her face as she retreated—her own hands swooping up to cover her cheeks, mouth, eyes, as shame and rage, guilt and disbelief rolled and swirled together in a primitive tide.

Rick registered all this, and his smile was sardonic, but not unkind. 'I suspect this is another gratification Saint Vanessa has been denying herself these past few years?'

'What?' It was no more than a whisper, but she understood him perfectly.

'I bet you were a little raver, up to eighteen years old. Since then, all that's gone by the board too, hasn't it—in the higher interests of duty and respectability?'

He was poignantly correct. Vanessa winced. No words came, but she backed away until she was safe in her chair again.

'Never mind.' Rick rose to his feet, stretched, and sauntered across the room to investigate her record collection. 'We've got plenty of time to put these things straight. Of course, some problems are easier to deal with than others. In the right hands, this particular area of martyrdom should soon be overcome. As for the rest, it's a bit more complex. We'll have to see what can be achieved.'

Vanessa was aware of a rising irritation. 'I suppose it goes without saying that the "right hands" are bound to be yours?'

'I'd be delighted if they were. Hey, keen on Haydn, aren't you? Have you got the *C major 'Cello Concerto*, by any chance?'

She stared, and glared. Irritation became fury, targeted on him, then rebounding back on herself. This was *so* ludicrous, it was positively funny. All over the wide world, thousands of females cherished fantasies of finding themselves in the arms of Rick Seymour. Now here was Vanessa Davies in that enviable situation, and as primly outraged as an elderly schoolma'am! Desperate not to do something she might regret—or *he* might—or...

They both had commitments, and she had moral values, even if he didn't. Oh yes, he was right: she was human, pulsating, passionate, no less than any other woman, probably more than some. She'd known that years ago—but he was right again there, too, sickeningly right. She'd kept it carefully smothered, since those carefree days as a very young girl, because . . .

Everyone knew why, and it was cruel of him to tempt her now, taunt her with her own nature. He was spoiled; used to playing with emotions and indulging those whims which ordinary people must keep under control. Used to picking up the toy that came to hand, then dropping it again. It was part of his creed, his world. He was an international star, after all, it was expected of him; he expected it of himself.

He turned away from her record shelf and stretched again, luxuriously, both arms high in the air, easily touching her low-beamed ceiling.

'I see you don't entirely dismiss jazz,' he remarked casually.

'No, I like some jazz very much. As long as it isn't too modern. My—my father was very keen on it.' She faltered, just slightly. 'This is really his collection . . . I kept it, and, well, I've learned to quite like it.'

'Good jazz has a lot in common with the best classical music.' Rick was accepting all this without irony, simply nodding his agreement. 'They're not separate disciplines, they're extensions of one another. And good rock's an extension of both,' he added lightly. Before she could argue, he went on, 'Who do you like? Any singers? Ella Fitzgerald? Bessie Smith?'

'Oh yes, both of those.' Vanessa was enthusiastic. 'They've got wonderful voices, so rich and expressive.'

Rick was leaning on the back of a chair now, watching her intently. She was gesturing emphatically. Then she caught herself out, and her hands dropped to her lap as she looked away.

He smiled, thoughtfully rubbing his chin with one hand. After a short pause, he said, 'So, how about this *Messiah*, then?'

'What? Oh!' In among all the rest, that initial bombshell had almost faded, but now it exploded all over again. 'I'll have to think about it.'

'You've got one hell of a lot of thinking to do.'

'Why? Oh, you mean about that, and...'

'And about Mark, yes.' He came out from behind the chair and took a step towards her. 'Don't keep us waiting too long, Vanessa. We're busy blokes, the vicar and I; we might change our minds if you dither. Neither of us can afford to hang about for ever.'

'I'm aware of that, and as far as I'm concerned...'

'For all you care, he can do without your services, and Mark can do without mine. I know, I know!' Rick chuckled, but his forehead creased— again that hint of weariness, perhaps stress. 'Give it a few days, that's all I ask. If I don't hear by— let's say the end of the week, I'll be in touch. OK?'

'It's likely to be no, on both counts.' Vanessa gripped the arms of her chair, fighting to steady her voice.

But Rick was striding over to her, grabbing her hands again and pulling her upright. She made to resist, but sheer shock was on his side.

Hands heavy on her shoulders, eyes searching her face, he followed up his advantage with a final, gentle exhortation.

'Don't be afraid of all this, Vanessa Davies. There's no harm in letting new views—clean air—

into a stale, stilted life. You're a great girl, and you're doing a great job. But you could use more humanity—do you know what I mean? Lord knows, I'm not perfect, but I believe in feelings and instinct. If you follow those, you won't go far wrong.'

But why should you care, thought Vanessa, bemused. Why should it concern you, whether I lack humanity or not?

'Vanessa,' he was continuing, 'couldn't you look on me as a catalyst? Don't fight all this, accept it. Let some changes in. You might be surprised,' he added, 'how much you can risk, and still not lose everything you've so laboriously built up.'

He knew just how afraid she was, but still he pressed her to take risks—as if his own happiness depended on her decisions, not just hers.

She stared back at him, floundering between hope and anxiety. 'I'll think about it,' she repeated finally. It was an incantation—a stylus stuck in a groove. Now she needed to be alone, to mull all this over.

'Please do that.' He was releasing her, reaching for his jacket, shrugging into it and zipping it up. 'But not for too long, eh? Now where did I dump my helmet? And the keys? And my gloves?' He went through into the hall. ''Bye now, Vanessa!' he called.

She did not answer, and he had not expected her to. She stood exactly where he had left her, while the front door slammed. Half a minute later, when the Moto-Guzzi throbbed into action and roared off round the corner, she was still standing there.

CHAPTER EIGHT

'DID you see the feature about Totem in the local paper?'

It was a casual enough question, through a mouthful of roast potato. Mark was staring blandly at the mound of food on his plate.

Vanessa went on eating her Sunday lunch, externally calm, inwardly tensing. He'd been surprisingly circumspect on this subject all week; not nagging, or even complaining, just coming out with the odd meaningful comment or long-suffering sigh. He hadn't forgotten and he didn't intend Vanessa to, either.

'Mr Scully asked me again about this Totem thing,' he had remarked, coming in from school on Tuesday.

'Everyone else in my tutor group did work experience, apart from me,' he lamented, after a chat on the telephone to Stewart on Thursday evening.

'If we don't make up our mind soon, it'll be too late, Scully reckons,' he announced, with a touch of petulance, on Friday.

Each time, Vanessa had fobbed him off with one of those 'we'll see' replies, which had been inadequate when he was twelve, and certainly did not fill the bill now. But over this issue she felt squeezed into the ultimate tight corner. So much more was at stake than Mark could possibly understand! If only she could explain it clearly—to herself, let alone to him! Not much chance of that: her head was too confused.

Here they were, past Rick's imposed deadline, and she hadn't moved an inch towards resolving either of those two decisions. Nor had she heard from Rick. She was suspended in a constant state of dithering apprehension.

Sometimes, in bed, fretting into the small hours, it all seemed ridiculously simple. Of course Mark should take advantage of this unusual opportunity! Why on earth not? He could hardly be scarred for life from contact with Rick's sort of music over a couple of days. And it would make him so happy; and might keep Rick quiet on that other, deeper challenge...

Then again, if she gave way over the one, wouldn't it be the thin end of the wedge—a step towards complying with the other? That prospect was altogether too terrifying. Daring to sing again— and in public! Re-opening those badly stitched wounds! It would be an appalling risk, yet at the same time the idea was enticing—exhilarating. How she had secretly longed for just such an event to sweep into her life, all those dogged, frustrated years!

But suppose she even contemplated it, what about the personal risk? There was no point in denying the profound effect Rick Seymour had on her. It wasn't just startling—it was total. No point, either, in trying to dismiss his impact, putting it down to fame and fortune, or popular acclaim. None of those considerations had ever cut the slightest ice with Vanessa, particularly as she had no time, and less inclination, for Rick's field of activity.

No, there was no ducking out of it: she was intimately hooked, a fish squirming on a baited line—and to a man who represented everything she considered trivial, ephemeral...

Or did she? How could she pretend to think that any more, now she had begun to know him? Witnessed him in action, this perceptive, intelligent, sensitive character? Oh yes, he was over-confident, even a bit on the arrogant side, but that was only to be expected in someone who had fought hard to reach a pinnacle, and had every intention of staying there, if not climbing higher.

None of this, of course, detracted from the central issue. Vanessa's thought-carousel returned to the same crunch, the same valid excuse for paralysis, over and over again. Rick Seymour was a happily married man. She had seen it with her own eyes, winced at it, even as she respected and envied it. So, he had to be using her—or worse, amusing himself with her. His interest had to be strictly temporary and selfish. Vanessa had suffered enough emotional deprivation, without throwing her heart into the ring, positively begging for more punishment.

There was no question, no argument. She must retreat—she must withdraw, completely, and at once...

'Vanessa! Did you hear me, or what? I said Totem was in the *Advertiser*!' Mark leaned across the table, his dark eyes reproachful.

'Yes, I heard. No, I didn't see it.'

'Don't you want to know what it says?'

'I have a strong suspicion you're about to tell me.'

'Actually, I do just happen to have it here.' Mark pushed his empty plate aside, reached under his chair and produced a folded newspaper. Ammunition, handily placed for the next salvo.

'Mark, please! Not while we're having lunch!'

'But we've finished! You've finished, haven't you?'

'Yes, but...'

'And so've I. It was great chicken, by the way. Thanks. So, if we've both finished, there's no problem, is there?'

Vanessa sighed. Not only had he physically outstripped her by seven inches, he was rapidly learning to gain the upper hand in other directions, too, through sheer force of charm and logic. Dangerous weapons: *male* charm, *male* logic. It wouldn't do.

She wasn't defeated, naturally, but she was biding her time. Now she leaned back, returning his limpid smile. 'Go on then—amaze me. Don't go thinking it'll break down my defences, though.'

'What do you mean?' Mark was a picture of injured innocence. 'I just thought you'd like to know, seeing as they've come to live here. Anyway, you're always saying you don't get time to read this paper, so I thought I might be doing you a favour.'

'Such generosity of spirit. Such striking unselfishness.'

Immune to her cynicism, Mark held up the folded page to show her the picture. There was the group: six heads, cleverly posed, faces spotlit, piled one above the other in a vertical line, their bodies invisible in shadow. A satisfying piece of design.

Rick's was at the top, half smiling, half frowning: enigmatic. Next came two other male faces—one West Indian, beaming widely; one white, bearded, rather dour, with long, straight hair. Then Ellie, endearingly cheerful as ever, complete with beads and dramatic make-up. Then two more men: the first with a lop-sided grin and a mass of dark curls, the second solemn and so close-cropped he looked almost bald.

'It's their latest record sleeve,' Mark enlightened her. 'They're meant to look like a totem pole, see?'

'I gathered that.' Vanessa was trying to take in every detail, without openly staring at the photograph.

'I'm saving to buy the album, then I'll be able to show you properly. This isn't a good reproduction, of course, being newsprint. The article's about them coming to live around here. Some people,' Mark added darkly, 'seem to think it's quite an honour.'

'No, really?'

Mark turned the paper round and began to read. Vanessa's attention was still on the picture, and she only half registered the words.

World famous group, Totem... taken up residence locally but we're sworn not to reveal where... intend to make their home in the area. New album *Dark Side of the Sun,* just out... title track, a tough rock ballad about the effects of drought on a peasant community, already been at Number One for three weeks... our picture shows, from the top, Rick Seymour, popularly recognised as the brain behind the band, plays mainly percussion and keyboards, writes all their songs and sings them; Win Jackson, bass, keyboards; Dave Hoyle, rhythm guitar,

vocals; Ellie Dale, bongos, vocals; Gideon
Imberg, tenor and alto saxophone; Victor
Delinsky, lead guitar and vocals...The ef-
fervescent Miss Dale, aka Mrs Imberg, tells
us that being the only female in this...

'What?' Suddenly Vanessa sat up and took
notice.

'Aka,' Mark explained. 'It means "also known
as". In other words, she's married to their sax
player, Gid Imberg. The one with the curls—see?
He's...'

'I know what it means.' Vanessa's voice emerged
sharp, yet hoarse and strangled. It seemed as if most
of her breath had been squashed from her body,
as if a ton weight had landed on her diaphragm.

Mark was side-tracked. 'Vanessa, are you OK?'
He put the newspaper down, peering at her more
closely. 'What's the matter?'

'I'm fine. It's nothing. A twinge of...'

She recovered some kind of outer composure, but
he went on staring at her, concerned. 'Twinge of
what? Was it anything I said?'

'Good lord, no, what gave you that idea?' She
cleared her throat. 'Indigestion, I expect. I told you
it was a mistake, throwing all this at me when we'd
hardly finished our meal.'

'I wasn't *throwing* it at you,' Mark muttered, torn
between guilt and exasperation. Sometimes his sister
was difficult to comprehend, and it wasn't as
though he didn't try to see things her way...up to
a point. 'I just thought you might like to know a
bit more about them.'

Vanessa had sipped some water, swallowed hard,
sat back on her chair and smoothed her hair from

her face with a hand that only shook very slightly.
Now she smiled at him. 'Fair enough. So, now I
know a bit more about them.' *More than you re-*
alise, my lad. 'What does that prove? Where does
that leave us?'

Mark shrugged, adolescent shoulders drooping.
'I don't know.' It had been a worthy effort, but
clearly unproductive—as he ought to have guessed
it would be—and now he slumped, dejected.

'I'll tell you where.' Suddenly Vanessa was all
vigour and animation. That moment of pain, or
panic, or whatever it was, had evidently passed, and
she was grinning at him, dark eyes shining. Almost
as if she'd had a piece of good news, rather than
a boring account of Totem and their latest activities, which Mark hadn't expected her to welcome
with cries of eager joy in any case.

He brooded at her again, suspicious this time.
'Where?'

'I've changed my mind. Don't ask me why, I just
have. It's a woman's prerogative, isn't it?'

Mark blinked. Was this the sister who was always
telling him off for falling into sexist stereotypes,
relying on masculine wiles and muscle, not treating
his girlfriends on an equal basis?

'I've decided. This silly business has gone on long
enough. It's not my responsibility to prevent you,
if you truly want to try something out, and a
genuine chance comes your way. I'm sorry, I've
been obstructive and negative. Of course you can
go, Mark. I'll give you a note for Mr Scully tomorrow. I—I might even phone Mr Seymour and
tell him myself.'

Her tone was clear and sure, her head high.
Mark's expression progressed wonderfully from

disbelief to astonishment to delight. 'Really? You *mean* this, Vanessa? But why? What made you...?'

'Never mind about that. Let's say it was—personal. There were things I didn't quite understand, which needed sorting out, and now I do. OK? No more questions?'

If Mark had any, he was wise enough not to push his luck by airing them. Instead he shot to his feet, came over to Vanessa, put an arm round her and planted a firm but clumsy kiss on her temple.

'Thanks, Ness,' he mumbled. When he stepped back, his cheeks were scarlet and his eyes misted. Vanessa's blurred in sympathy. The bond between the two of them was easing, maturing—yet it had never been stronger. Not just because Mark had got his own way—there was more to it than that—something to do with her own new self-awareness, these inner shifts she had been experiencing recently.

Mark had no way of knowing the facts, but he did have an intuitive perception of their importance. If it made Vanessa happy, whatever it was, he was glad—for her sake as well as his. She deserved to be happy. He often wished *he* could provide her with more joy, but somehow...

'You can make the arrangements with Mr Scully, can't you? And Rick too, if necessary?' she was saying now.

Mark was intrigued. *Rick?* What was going on behind his back?

'Right.' He started stacking crockery, covertly watching her.

Vanessa emptied some scraps into the kitchen bin. 'By the way, did you know he drives a powerful motorbike?'

'Rick Seymour? *Really?* What make? How powerful?'

'I don't know how many cc's it's got, but it's called Moto...'

'Moto-Guzzi?' Mark supplied, when she paused to recollect the word.

'That's the one. It's an impressive-looking beast, I'm sure he'll show you.'

'Oh, you've seen it, have you? How come?' He gaped.

'I've had some business dealings with the man, remember? Now, if I'm not wrong, it's your turn to wash up. I think I'll go and sit in there, and finish reading this, if you don't mind.'

'Course I don't mind. I'll bring you some coffee in a minute.'

'Lovely. Thanks.' Vanessa grabbed the newspaper and marched through to the sitting-room.

Mark hummed the title track from *Dark Side Of The Sun* as he squirted far too much detergent into the bowl and frothed it up into rich suds. Vanessa was full of mysteries and unexpected twists. At least living with her wasn't dull, especially at the moment. He couldn't wait to tell Stewart: in fact, he'd get on the phone to him as soon as he'd done this...or perhaps go round there...

He glanced over his shoulder to where his sister, at the other end of the long room, was deeply engrossed in the local rag. If that ordinary publication was such a magic tonic, he wished she'd read it from cover to cover, every week. But he was far too pleased with her—and with himself—to say so.

When Mark came home on Monday, Vanessa was busy in the kitchen.

'You look smug! Talk about the cat that found the butter!'

'I've had a good day, thanks for asking. I got an A-minus for that English Lit. essay, the Shakespeare one, remember?'

'The one I helped you with, about Lady Macbeth? Well done, Mark! That's good news!'

'Yeah.' He dumped his bag, and came to sit at the table. 'Brilliant, aren't we? Any tea in the pot?'

'There could be, if you put some there.'

'Right.' He got up again and reached for the tea jar. 'Oh, and Mr Scully was really chuffed about the work experience. He says he's sure you've made the right decision and you won't regret it.'

'Oh, that's what he says, is it?'

'He sends you his best wishes, and hopes to meet you one day.'

'Charmed, I'm sure.' Vanessa scrubbed at a greasy patch of sink.

'There's one thing, Ness. He says we ought to make the arrangements ourselves, seeing as it's so local, and you've got in with Totem...'

'I most certainly have not *got in with* Totem! I happen to have met two of them, in the line of my work. That's all.'

'Well, if you wouldn't mind giving Rick Seymour a call—I mean, at least you've met him—I mean, he might not know who I was, if I did it...'

'Oh, he'd know who you were, Mark. He knows all about you.'

'What, even my name?' The thought seemed awe-inspiring.

'Your name's been coming up with monotonous regularity, if you want to know, in every one of our conversations. Then there's Ron Scully's machinations. I'm surprised Rick isn't fed up to the back teeth with the whole idea, but apparently he isn't. For reasons best known to himself, he's keen on inviting you to worship at his feet. I can't think why,' she lied, 'but there you are.'

'OK, so will you . . . ?'

Vanessa frowned. Rick was due to contact her anyway; overdue, in fact. When he did, she might as well raise this subject. After all, it had been her change of heart: it was up to her to see it through.

'I'll see what I can do, Mark. I'll be in touch with him soon.'

Mark poured the tea. 'You're being great about this, you know, Vanessa. Thanks a lot.'

'Yes, I am, aren't I? Don't mention it, ratface. Have some of Carol's flapjack. It's good and chewy, the way you like it.'

Whistling Mozart's *First Horn Concerto* through her teeth, she embarked on weighing potatoes for tomorrow's order. Assorted salads, various. For how many people—six? Three pounds should be enough.

'After that,' she went on, 'if you've got homework to do, get out from under my feet and do it. If you haven't, go and find something else. If you can't think of anything useful, I've got a pile of vegetables to chop, or you could wash up these pots . . .'

'I've got loads of homework,' Mark assured her hastily. Grabbing his tea, and three chunks of flapjack, he beat a speedy retreat.

Rick did not telephone that day, or the next. By Wednesday evening, Vanessa was forced to admit she was on tenterhooks. First she wondered when the promised call would come. Then she wondered *if* it would come. All the time, she wondered how she would deal with it, if and when it came. Her determination wasn't weakening, exactly; but it was being stretched thin by this prolonged delay.

What was the man playing at? Was he deliberately testing her out? Or had he simply forgotten? Had his involvement been so superficial, after all, and now he was regretting it? Fine, so he wasn't married—or not to Ellie, at least—but that didn't mean he was free to sport, as and when he chose, with any woman who took his fancy...in a way, it meant he was *less* free...somehow, instinctively, Vanessa knew him to be too serious and straight for such games. This news seemed to have clicked the whole scene into a different perspective. There was a certain mutual trust at work here, and she would make room for it.

It was a positive, spirited decision; but it didn't stop her guessing, agonising over the possibilities until they threatened to reach obsession point.

On Thursday—grasping her courage, along with the receiver—she dialled the private number for the old manor. If Mohammed refused to come to the mountain...

'Oh—er—hello. Could I speak to Rick Seymour, please?'

'Sorry, he's not here.' It was a voice she didn't recognise: broadly local, female, middle-aged. The efficient housekeeper, no doubt.

'Oh. Er—what about Ellie Dale, then?'

'No, dear, they're all away. On tour, round the provinces, then London, promoting their new album.'

It was said with an air of pride and a kind of stiffness, as if the lady was quoting someone else's unfamiliar phrases.

'I see.' There was no reason for Vanessa to feel so jolted. This was part of their job, not only making records, but taking the real live music to the real live audiences—just like any other musicians—she knew that. 'Did he—how long are they expected to be away, do you know?'

'It'll be ten days altogether. Eight concerts, in eight cities. They'll be back on Monday, and then they'll need a few days' rest before the final—er—gig, in Bristol next weekend.

'Ah. OK then, I'll try again after that.'

'Any message, dear? Can I help at all? A booking, was it?'

'No, it's all right, thanks. At least...' Vanessa hesitated. 'You could just say that Vanessa Davies rang, and she's decided to...'

'Miss Davies! Oh, it's you, is it? You should've said! He left a message for you—let me see—I'm sure I've got it here...'

'A message for me?'

'That's right, dear. Hold on...I know it's here...Mr S was just leaving, and he remembered three different important things, in case people rang, and he told me all of them at once, and I jotted them down straight away, on this...yes, here we are!'

The woman coughed importantly. '"If Miss V Davies rings, tell her Mr S is sorry he didn't get round to contacting her when he said...this tour put everything else out of his mind...it's been— What's this word—frantic? Yes, that's it—frantic here, all week. But he has got something important to say to her, and he'll be in touch when he gets back.'' There you are dear. Does that make sense to you?'

'Make sense? Oh, yes, I suppose it does. Thank you very much. I'll wait to hear from him, then.' Was this heaviness in her limbs relief, or disappointment, or neither, or both?

'Hang on a moment, dear. That's not quite all. There's another bit.'

'Oh yes?'

'It's scribbled at the bottom—honestly, I must do something about my writing—"Please tell Miss Davies he'll probably be sleeping off the effects of the tour all day Tuesday, but if she wants a proper chat, she could meet him at the church——" that'll be St Saviour's, dear, in the village "—Wednesday evening. It's the first rehearsal of the——" what's this? "—Handel, and she might like to listen." Got all that, dear?' the good lady added, as a dense silence greeted this gem, from Vanessa's end of the line.

'Oh yes, I've got it all. Thank you very much.'

'Wednesday evening. If you wanted to know the exact time, dear, you could always ask the vicar. It's got something to do with him, this Handel thing, I'm sure.'

'I believe so. I'll bear it in mind.' Vanessa's voice was prim and starchy. It was hardly this lady's fault, but she couldn't help her reaction. 'I won't bother you with a return message. You've been most kind.'

''Tis what I'm here for, my dear. I'll just say you rang then, shall I? Not whether you'll be there or not?'

'I doubt whether I'll be there.' Vanessa was positively rigid. 'But do say I rang, yes, thank you.'

'Goodbye now,' the lady said, but Vanessa was already ringing off.

She stomped through to the kitchen, where she attacked an innocent lump of dough—kneading it with ten times the necessary energy. She was seething, with a potent blend of indignation and curiosity. Something important to tell her—that was the bait. Meet him at the church—first Handel rehearsal—that was the trap. How bland it sounded, how simple—uncomplicated—convenient!

Only the two of them, he and she, understood the true depth of that challenge. 'She might like to listen!' How devious men's minds were—and yet how transparent!

She would not go back on her promise to Mark; that would be grossly unfair. She'd give the residents of the manor time to get safely home and sleep off their strenuous week—then she'd give Rick a call, tell him her decision about Mark, make the arrangements, and hear whatever it was he had to say to her. Whatever could it be?

As for his other proposition: it was out of the question, as he well knew! An insult—damn cheek—a diabolical liberty! He *knew* how she felt! The very *idea* that she might so much as set foot in the church when all that was going on, raking up old aches, so laboriously healed...

And he was so obvious! Did he take her for a fool? It was all very well, luring her there with hints of further communication, but surely he realised she'd see through his ruse? If once she heard that music—saw Rick and Ellie, and the rest, participating—they both knew how tempted she'd be to crack, give way, join in...

No chance! His claim to understand her was way out of line, if he assessed her to be so malleable—so easily influenced ...

She shaped the dough into a neat ball and left it to prove again. Time to grit her teeth, sharpen her wits—and get on with the ordinary business of living, taking the days as they came, one by one.

CHAPTER NINE

HERE she stood again, outside St Saviour's at dusk. There had been showers all day, and now the evening was freshened with the smell of damp country soil.

Vanessa stared up at the tower. Surely it moved—floated—against the billowing sky? Immediately above one corner, an elusive crescent moon sheened in and out of the racing cloud-masses.

Out here it was serene, but what was going on in there?

The windows were brightly lit, shedding colourful patterns through stained glass. At first Vanessa could hear nothing; then she stepped nearer and could just detect a flow of thin, pure notes. Subtle, not strident. No voices, only this single line of melody, woven with gentle harmony.

It came from the organ; therefore, presumably, it came from Rick's hands. Vanessa tensed, picturing those fingers on the keys, feeling them as vividly as if her own flesh was the keyboard itself, responsive to every nuance, each possessive demand they made as they strayed over its surface...

She stiffened her resolve yet again. Up to half an hour ago she had definitely not been intending to show up at this rehearsal. She had left the house on foot, telling herself she simply needed a few minutes' air and exercise. Setting out had had no connection with the imperious Seymour summons. She hadn't even bothered to find out what time this thing started. There was no point, if she wasn't going.

But her feet had obviously had other ideas. Deep in thought, she had paid little attention to where they led her. Fifteen minutes later, here she was, lurking in the churchyard, hovering in the porch. Dithering over whether to take the plunge after all, or take to her heels.

It was not an edifying sight. She was glad no one else could see it, least of all Rick. She pulled herself up straight, shoulders back, chin high. Her feet had more sense, and more pride, than her head! Shirking challenges had never been her way, and now she was here, she might as well slip in to watch and listen for a while from the back. Rick wouldn't even see her, busy in his niche. With luck, no one else would notice either, and she really was curious to hear Ellie singing... hear Rick playing again...

She recognised the piece as soon as she pushed open the heavy doors. It was the Pastoral Symphony, an interlude between vocal solos and choruses. *The Messiah* might be accompanied by a small group of players, or a simple orchestra, or just piano, or organ. In this case, the whole responsibility lay with Rick. Judging by this example, he was fulfilling it expertly, with delicate confidence and competence, utterly in keeping with the spirit of the music; no less than Vanessa would have expected.

Everyone else in the church appeared spellbound, eyes turned towards the organ pipes, ears glued to the sounds emerging from them. The vicar sat with his choirmaster among the choir, exuding approval. A few faces Vanessa knew, and some she didn't; a few bejeaned figures sprawling on front pews—no doubt members of the Totem entourage, loyally supporting this local event, as their leader instructed. Yes, there was Ellie, sitting close to the curly character from the photograph—her husband, Gideon...

Vanessa's head reeled, her stomach clenched with recalled foolishness—and a new wave of panic. She was crazy to be in here! She must escape, while there was still time... she must pull the door open, slide out, and no one would ever be the wiser...

Just as she began turning the handle the Symphony drew to its end. The enrapt audience waited for the last trill, the final elongated phrase to fade away. Then they came to life, shifting and muttering, radiating pleasure. As if on a direct signal, Ellie glanced over to the door—and spotted Vanessa. At once she grinned and waved, at the same time leaning to whisper in Gid's ear. Then he looked up too, smiling and nodding.

Vanessa was trapped. She could hardly cut and run, not now. With a brief return wave, she sidled to the back of the church. It was relatively dim there, and she could sit still and quiet in the shadows and watch the proceedings.

A fond hope! The Reverend Harte was not likely to ignore anyone entering his domain. He had seen her, and was already homing in down the side aisle.

Vanessa moved to meet him—reluctant, yet accepting the inevitable. Was all this pre-ordained, or was she here of her own free will? It wasn't quite the moment for such theological debate, even it if was a highly suitable place. Just now, she suspected, she was about to require all her wits and strength of mind.

'Vanessa! How very nice to see you here!'

She found herself smiling shyly back. 'I wasn't sure I'd be able...'

'Then you found you had a bit of spare time? That's splendid!' He was making it easier for her, she knew that. He was a plain, pleasant man, with keen grey eyes and a sharp understanding of human nature. Vanessa liked him, but found him slightly intimidating.

'I thought I'd just see how it was—how you were...'

'It's going well. Rick's doing wonderful things, as you'll have heard. The rest of us are—what shall I say?—feeling our way. Most of the choir have sung this before, of course, and George will be drilling them on their own in his usual merciless style. What I was really hoping for tonight was a bash at some of those solos. How did George put it? Test the acoustic, along with the new talent. George was sceptical about our newcomers,' the vicar explained affably. 'Better the devil you know, he said to me. And I said, O ye of little faith.' He chuckled. 'And I was right. Anyway, Vanessa, we're specially glad to see you, because...'

On a cold instinct, she was retreating. 'I'm here to listen, vicar.'

'Oh, quite. Quite. Rick did mention it, and I appreciate how you feel—how you've always felt about singing in public. Absolutely.'

In the background, Rick had struck up on the organ again, and the choirmaster had got his straggling charges to their collective feet. Now the rousing strains of *And He Shall Purify* echoed to the arches. It was sounding good already; distinct possibilities were taking shape. No wonder the vicar was smug.

They both listened for a minute, then Vanessa murmured, 'I suppose I might join in with some of the chorales...'

To be honest, her vocal chords were tingling. Her throat seemed to tremble, with a long-delayed yearning for action. Rick had known this would happen, and underneath, so had she. Exposing herself to this music, this sense of creative co-operation—remembering how it used to be—how it could have been; absorbing this atmosphere, these vibrations...

The experience was profound. Even stronger than the self-induced resentment which had paralysed her all these years. That harsh bitterness was on the wane, as she secretly suspected it had been for some time. In its place surged this craving, a physical appetite, cruelly suppressed.

The vicar was leaning nearer, to pick up her words. If he guessed how deep her reactions were, he gave no sign. 'You're welcome to join the choir any time, you know that, Vanessa. George is always complaining he needs more dainty ladies to balance his booming gents.'

Vanessa returned his smile. The choirmaster was an elderly ex-schoolteacher who took his role seriously, with excellent results.

'Perhaps I might, then.' She was relaxing, as the vicar carefully took the pressure off. 'If it helps George out, in his soprano line...'

'Why not? No, all I was going to say was that we haven't actually found a soprano soloist yet. We're on to several possibles,' the vicar said nonchalantly, 'but none of them could confirm by tonight, so we've been making do with just the other three. It's no problem, except we've struck one slight—er—difficulty.'

'Oh yes?' Vanessa eyed him. It wasn't charitable to be suspicious of a man of the cloth. But then again, he was a man.

'You see, Miss Dale—Ellie, you know, from Totem?'

'Yes, I know Ellie.'

'Well, she turns out—rather to my surprise, I'll admit, and even more to George's—to be a fine natural contralto. A beautifully simple rendering she gave us earlier, of *Oh Thou That Tellest*. Quite touchingly unspoiled.' The vicar sighed, enjoying the recollection.

'I gathered she was—flexible, in her talents.' Vanessa tried to sound less dry. Surely she could afford to be generous about Ellie, especially now?

'Exactly. As is her colleague, Rick Seymour—an impressive young man. Displays unprecedented versatility and depth of interpretation—so George assures me,' he told her gravely.

'I expect George is right.' Vanessa wished he'd get to the point. 'What does all this have to do with me?'

'Ellie was extremely keen to try the aria she knows best, which happens to be *He Shall Feed His Flock*. But she can't, because . . .'

Vanessa was ahead of him. 'Because it's a duet, with the soprano.'

'Precisely!' The vicar was admiring. 'You must know the work rather well! Have you sung in it, by any chance?'

'Parts of it. We studied it at school. I've got a marvellous recording of it at home. Anyway, all singers know it quite well . . .'

All would-be singers, she should have said. She stared away, out of a window. It was only too clear where all this had been leading. Ellie must be in the plot as well. Vanessa was pale and impassive, but her mind was whirring, as violent new urges clashed with the stale familiar habit of self-protection. The vicar had done no more than pinpoint her extreme conflict; he certainly had not perpetrated it.

Now he was taking the plunge, calm and friendly. 'You wouldn't consider trying out that one piece, would you? It would be a real favour to us all. It's such a lovely melody, and no member of the choir seems willing or able to take it on, and Ellie's disappointed...'

'What makes you think *I'm* willing or able?' Vanessa snapped.

The vicar hesitated, contemplating his well-polished shoes. Then he quietly replied, 'Intuition suggests you're able. Optimism allows me to hope you might be willing. Nothing more.' She said nothing, so he continued. 'No strings attached, as they say. Just to do us this one good turn. We intend to have tracked down another candidate before the next rehearsal, if you don't...'

'I'll do it.'

The decision was reached exactly as she spoke the words. It was impossible to tell who was the more startled, herself or the Reverend Harte.

'Excellent! Ellie will be delighted, and so will George. It'll give him a chance to assess this soprano acoustic.'

It was all so matter-of-fact. No mention of Rick, or the deeper implications... keeping it functional, probably wisely. The vicar was already leading the way to the front of the church, and Vanessa slowly followed. Events had taken her over—but instead of fear, she was aware of a sense of release. Better not think too hard; better just go with it, see what happened.

The vicar arrived well ahead, with his long strides. The chorale had finished, and he went straight to George for a private word. Then, while George disappeared to consult Rick, the vicar crossed to tell Ellie, where she sat with Gideon, and the tenor and bass soloists.

Ellie bounced to meet Vanessa, grinning happily. 'Vanessa, this is great! I've been dying to have a go at that song—I think it's fabulous—and it's the one I know best. But it's no good without the other part, is it?'

'No.' Vanessa was wry, but it was hard to be unaffected by Ellie's exuberance. Her own excitement was swelling: a peppering of nerves, a thrill of anticipation.

Ellie drew nearer and lowered her tone. 'I realise what this means to you, Vanessa. I haven't forgotten, and neither has Rick.' She waved a vague hand at the organ loft, a stark, unconscious reminder that Rick was only yards away—perhaps viewing most of this in his little mirror—definitely knowing what was going on.

From this angle Vanessa couldn't see the mirror, and she deliberately avoided shifting to where she could. At this moment, one glance from those penetrating blue eyes would surely finish her off. No, she would stay out of his range. This watershed in her life was private, even though it was so public. It had nothing to do with Rick Seymour—unless it had everything to do with him?

Now he was playing the last few bars of the preceding aria, and Ellie was leading Vanessa to stand beside her on the altar steps. George was handing her a copy of the score, open at the right page, and it seemed hundreds of pairs of eyes were on her, hundreds of pairs of ears straining for her every faltering note, judging, critical...

Two, three seconds of sheer blind, deaf, dumb terror, while Rick gave Ellie her opening chord; then Ellie was off on her recitative: *Then shall the eyes of the blind be opened, and the ears of the deaf unstoppéd; then shall the lame man leap as an hart, and the tongue of the dumb shall sing...*

They were right, all of them: Ellie was a marvellous, mellifluous alto. Untainted by exaggerated sophistication, smoothly true to the note. *The tongue of the dumb shall sing.* How strangely apposite, those immortal words! Vanessa's heart lifted as Ellie phrased them.

Now Ellie and Rick progressed to the main Air. Such a richly satisfying tune, and she sang it with a fresh vigour which heightened Vanessa's own energy. But there was this drum of tension, wickedly beating, far within—threatening to overcome her instinctive response to the music...

He shall feed his flock like a shepherd...and gently lead those that are with young.

A few linking bars; one of Handel's neat key changes; then Ellie was stepping slightly back, with a quick, reassuring squeeze of Vanessa's arm. Rick was firmly playing the soprano introduction. It was her turn. Now, or never. Never! *Never!*

She moved back half a pace, as if to flee. The door was over there. She could be through it in a couple of seconds...

Suddenly, she knew this was not the way. It must be now, not never. Now! *Now!*

Come unto Him, all ye that labour...

She was so rusty, like an unoiled hinge. How had she had the gall to rant at Rick for actually *using* his skills? She had a lot to learn, but she was starting; this would be a start...

Come unto Him ye that are heavy laden, and He will give you rest.

It was getting better. She could feel this new energy—no, not new, magically restored, pouring through the opened barriers, making up for a little of the lost time. Like a powerful river, dammed for years, pushing its path to the sea. Now it was on course again, there would be no stopping it... No more artificial gates...

Take His yoke upon you and learn of Him, for He is meek and lowly of heart, and ye shall find rest unto your souls.

The phrases rose, fell and repeated. Now her voice was soaring, sweet and clear. Rick's accompaniment was perfect—sensitive, supportive, but not intrusive. She could feel him with her, all the way. Even as she drowned in her own experience of making the music, she was alert to his share in it. The triumph belonged to them both, equally. This jubilation flowed from his hands, to her voice, back and forth, mutually expressive.

Her solo was over, and Rick was rounding it off in that inimitable style she recognised—positive, yet understated. She lowered her copy of the score and stepped back beside Ellie, whose arm immediately crept round her waist in a spontaneous salutation.

The silence seemed eternal, but was only a few moments. Nobody clapped, or made a fuss. One did not applaud in religious oratorios, especially at the first rehearsal. Already they were pressing on with the next job. There was plenty to be done yet, and they all had homes and families to return to.

But when Vanessa's eyes had demisted and she glanced round, she saw that the bustle was not all it had seemed. The vicar was looking in her direction, his face registering warm sympathy and personal pleasure. George the choirmaster was gazing at her in undisguised amazement, as were half his choir. Gid was grinning, sharing the achievement along with his pride in Ellie.

Ellie's arm stayed round her as they walked back to the others. When she faced Vanessa, tears stood at the corners of her eyes. Vanessa was the one who smiled weakly, digging her in the ribs.

'Cut that out! Your warpaint will run!'

Ellie's normal grin returned at once. 'Dead right it will, and I take hours getting this mascara on. What's more, I never cry. It's all your fault, Vanessa Davies!' Gid was standing up as they approached. 'Come and meet my lovely Gid.' Ellie caught hold of his hand. 'Gid, this is Vanessa.'

'I feel as if we've met, somehow.' Gid's smile was as ready as his wife's, but his eyes were solemn.

'Me, too.' Vanessa smiled back.

'Nice work, girls,' Gid said, as they all sat down. The tenor and bass soloists leaned across to add their congratulations. Vanessa began to feel distinctly euphoric.

George clapped his hands for their attention, and the mutter of conversation gradually ebbed. 'That was a delightful surprise, I'm sure we'll all agree. A charming performance by both young ladies. Miss Davies, you have been hiding your light under a bushel—to coin a phrase.' There was a polite titter of laughter. George might be pompous and whimsical, but he was popular. 'Might we prevail on you to make your contribution more permanent?'

Vanessa reddened and stared down at her hands. 'I—I don't know.'

Prompted by a warning glare from the vicar, George did not persist. 'At any rate, perhaps you'd consider helping us out with one or two more solo spots, just for this evening? As you're here, and in such excellent voice?'

'Of course.' She looked up now, controlling the flustered moment. One step at a time, they ought to understand that. She might be learning to crawl again, but it was too soon to ask her to run.

The next hour seemed to contract to minutes. Vanessa hadn't been so happy for a long time: happy to be singing, and to be involved in making music with other people. Happy with her unbelievable breakthrough; happy in Ellie and Gid's cheerful company.

The tenor and bass displayed their prowess in two arias each, and the choir had a commendable stab at another chorus. Ellie sang another solo with no less verve, and then it was Vanessa's turn again.

She didn't baulk or dither. She accepted the invitation, standing alone this time, and simply gave of her best. Her confidence was rapidly returning. It needed a lot of practice and polish, of course, but the facility was there. Like swimming, or cycling—once you mastered it, you never really forgot the knack.

Then it was nine-thirty, and suddenly everyone was pressing to be off. Ellie and Gid made their excuses and disappeared to a late dinner date, with smiles and hugs all round. Vanessa sat on, oddly becalmed among the busy tying of ends, planning, arranging, discussing. No one pestered her. Either they were too discreet or too preoccupied, but they left her alone with her reflections.

Rick stayed put at his post, continuing to play. Somehow she fancied he knew she was still there, listening, and calming herself down. He gave them a reprise of the Pastoral Symphony, a rendition of the Overture, and then, as the church emptied, he burst into a dynamic overflow—one of those cascading, crashing toccatas.

Vanessa understood. He'd held this virtuoso power in check all evening, disciplined to the decorous niceties of Handel. Now he had to let go and redress the balance before calling it a day.

The last cadences and chords died away. When Rick finally emerged from his corner, the only ones left were Vanessa and the vicar.

Rick stretched every inch of his body and shook his head vehemently. 'That's better! Been cooped up in there a bit too long!' He closed his eyes, then turned them full on Vanessa, smiling.

The vicar was hurrying over to him. 'Wonderful, Rick! You're not going to need much practice! You appear to be note-perfect already. I think this is going to be a success, thanks to you.'

'I enjoy it, vicar—I told you, I'm pleased to do it, and so is Ellie. So are we all.' Rick looked from the vicar to Vanessa, sitting quietly in her front pew. There was no surprise in his face, but a penetrating warmth. He had expected her to turn up here tonight; now he expected her to be still here, waiting. She should feel angry—but she didn't. 'Aren't we, Vanessa?' he added, lightly.

She cleared her throat. 'I enjoyed it.' She was a bit gruff, but her eyes were as bright as his.

'Well, we do appreciate it. You'll be wanting to get off now, and I promised Margaret I wouldn't be too late. But I'll be on to you very soon about the next stage, Rick, if that's all right?'

'That's fine, vicar. We'll be on our way, shall we, Vanessa?'

'Oh—yes.' She got to her feet. Suddenly she felt drained, and stunned.

The vicar was tactfully avoiding any suggestion of her future participation, though all three of them knew they were thinking of it. He ushered them out of the church, still enthusing.

'Such an inspired work, *The Messiah*, I always think.'

'I always think so, too.' As if sensing Vanessa's weariness, Rick took her arm. She welcomed the gesture, as naturally as it had been offered. 'Cheerio then, vicar. Keep in touch!'

'I certainly will. Thanks again, both of you. Take care!'

'Goodbye!' On the steps, Vanessa turned to wave. The Reverend Harte stood at his church door, pensively watching them go.

Rick was not the man for unnecessary post mortems. He said not a word about the developments of the last couple of hours. He simply steered her towards the car park.

There was one large car in it. Rick stopped, looked at it, then at Vanessa. 'Didn't you drive?'

'I walked.' She paused before adding sardonically, 'I wasn't intending to come. I sort of—found myself here.'

'I see.' In the darkness, she knew he was grinning.

'You knew I'd be here, didn't you, Rick?' There was no rancour in the question, and he answered it with an equally straight statement.

'I hoped you would, Vanessa.'

'Thanks.' Under cover of night, she whispered the one, significant syllable.

His arm tightened through hers at once. 'No, Vanessa. Thank *you*. It was a truly moving moment, and I won't forget it. I suspect you won't, either?' He glanced down at her in the gloom.

'Not likely!' The silence they shared was easy, under the silver glimmer of that slice of moon. After a while, she ventured, 'Is this your car, then?'

'It is. I'll give you a lift. Good job I brought one of the BMWs instead of the bike, isn't it? Good job it was a wet evening, eh, Vanessa?'

She only smiled at his teasing. 'I've walked home this late before.'

'Well, you're not going to now.' He released her arm to search in his pocket for the car keys. 'To tell the truth, I didn't fancy being cluttered up with helmets and all that.' He was unlocking the passenger side, seeing her in, slamming the door, then climbing in beside her.

Then they were purring unostentatiously through the lamplit village. Vanessa leaned back against the plush upholstery, wishing this ride might go on for ever—intimate, undemanding, suspended...

'The others were going to some jamboree or other, as soon as they got away.' His voice was soft, but it cut into her reverie.

'So Ellie and Gid said. Didn't you want to go too?'

'Who said I wasn't?' He grinned round at her, changing gear on a steep slope. 'Actually, I'm not.

I don't feel like it. And anyway, you haven't forgotten I've got something to tell you?'

'Of course not.' Foolishly, she *had* forgotten. 'That's what I'm here for, really, isn't it? You'd better tell me now.'

Instead of answering, he hesitated. Then he said, 'If I'm going to explain properly, I need to show you something, too. Have you got a few minutes? Can you come up to the manor, or should you get straight home to Mark? We could have a drink, or a cup of coffee...'

Mark—that reminded her! Reality was flooding back, after the living fantasies of this evening. 'Mark won't worry. He was out when I left, and he'll expect me when he sees me. Yes, I could do with a drink, thank you. And actually...' she paused, savouring the thought of his pleasure when he heard it, 'I've got something to tell you, too.'

'Is that right?' He swung the sleek car round a sharp bend—away from the route to her house, following the road out to his.

'That's right.' Something in his tone alerted her, jerked her out of the euphoria. She was deliberately entering *his* territory, on *his* terms. Best to make sure they were her terms, as well...

She sat up straighter as he turned through the gates, up the drive, and drew to a smooth halt in the yard. Then he switched the engine off, and the lights, smiling at her in the shadows.

'Here was I, thinking the excitements of this evening were over, when apparently they're only just starting.'

Vanessa hoped her breezy laugh was more convincing than it felt.

CHAPTER TEN

THE manor was dark and quiet. Outside, rolling lawns and fields were silvery grey, rather than green, in the moonlight. Inside, an orderly peace reigned: signs of efficient domestic organisation as well as some fast and furious professional renovation.

Rick led Vanessa through the tidy kitchen, round those same corners, down those same passages as last time. Newly carpeted and decorated, his own domain was now securely enclosed behind its own entrance.

No one intrudes... yes, he preferred to keep his autonomy and privacy, as well as his own counsel. Physically, as well as spiritually, he was independent.

'We've really got on with it, since your last visit,' he remarked, switching on lights, and unlocking doors.

'It looks very smart.'

'Ellie had some say in the colour scheme. She's got a good eye.'

'Ah, yes.' Vanessa stopped in her tracks, overwhelmed by a new dilemma. Should she confess to him now her foolish misconception about himself and Ellie? Or should she wait till later?

'Bathroom's in here, remember?' He tapped the door as they were passing it.

'I remember.' She hurried to catch him up. She'd tell him later, when she was more relaxed and confident. Just now, she was concentrating on letting this strange new trust in, feeling it stir, hoping it would develop.

'I insisted on my own hospitality area,' he was declaring now. 'I have all the gear—microwave, fridge-freezer, drinks cabinet...'

He ushered her into a freshly painted suite which she had not seen before. A small private lounge, stylishly simple. Through an interconnecting door, she caught a glimpse of bedroom, similarly furnished. Modern and classical prints on plain walls; thick, unfussy rugs on parquet floors. The Seymour taste was characteristic and clear: elegantly functional.

'I didn't realise you had all this, too. I thought it was just your study.' She stood, staring round. 'It's really nice, Rick.'

'You didn't see the half of it. When you last came, all this was still under dustsheets. Now— coffee, or something stronger? I'm going to indulge in a spot of vodka, myself.'

'Yes please. Good and long, with plenty of tonic, if you've got it.' She allowed herself a moment of surprise at her own lack of hesitation. She hardly ever drank spirits, let alone vodka. But then, she was doing all sorts of things she hardly ever did.

'I've got it. And I've got lemon, I've got ice, I've got olives, and cherries in jars, and little sticks to spear them with. You name it, I've got it.' He was busy with the fridge and cupboard. 'Ice?'

'Definitely.' She was studying a pair of abstract wood carvings on a shelf. When he approached, she was absorbed, unaware of his soft shoes padding across the rug. For a few seconds he stood behind her, looking over her shoulder, then he touched her arm softly and handed her the drink.

Swinging round, she stepped back—then took it, relaxing, relishing that chill smoothness of frosted glass against her warm palm.

'Thanks.' She smiled. 'I need this. Singing's thirsty work.'

'Cheers!' He returned the smile, clinking his glass on hers. They both sipped, still contemplating each other thoughtfully.

Vanessa broke the link, turning away and clearing her throat. 'This really is all so smart, Rick. I'm impressed.'

'Wait till you see next door!'

Vanessa was intrigued by his expression of gleeful pride, like a schoolboy with a new toy.

'Next door? You mean, the bedroom, or the office I saw last time?'

'Neither of those. Something else.' He drank some more, then he was grabbing her free hand, suddenly impatient, pulling her into the corridor and in through the opposite door. 'Come on, I'll show you now.'

Vanessa fixed her mind on not spilling her drink on the new carpet. Anything, rather than realise the full impact of that forceful grasp, those hard, cool fingers wrapped around hers, that body, drawing hers.

It was a tiny room, with one window behind a venetian blind. It was starkly utilitarian, containing only a moulded plastic desk, a plush swivel chair, and a whole wall bristling with hardware. Screens and printers, a console of switches and knobs, a keyboard, and three shining new metal filing cabinets among the electronic machinery.

'Good grief!' Vanessa stared. 'It's like the inside of a space ship!'

'This is my latest technology; the nerve centre of my operations.' Rick made a grand, sweeping gesture with his hand—which happened to be still attached to hers.

She caught her drink in the nick of time, then drank a lot more of it, before he could make any more unexpected movements. Evidently he was waiting for her to comment, but what was there to say about a computer? When you'd seen one, in her humble, ignorant opinion, you'd seen them all. 'Very impressive, Rick,' she said at last.

He dropped her hand, turning to face her, and she was relieved to find him grinning. 'Don't tell me you're out of tune with this age of the automaton?'

'Out of tune? Yes, you could put it that way. But I can see this all very—very useful.' She paused. 'Er—what do you plan to use it for?'

He walked across to the keyboard, running a finger over the keys as if he expected musical notes to emerge. 'If you knew the complexity of Totem's organisation, Vanessa, you wouldn't ask. This pretty baby should take care of all those boring, vital, time-consuming administrative details which drive me mad. Hiring, firing, booking, recording, scheduling. Doing the accounts, getting and spending. Equipment, places, people, transport, dates, venues—for years ahead. It can store lyrics, and even musical scores!' This was the final marvel; he paused to let Vanessa appreciate it.

'All the things you insist on doing because you won't delegate?'

'I prefer to entrust responsibility to a proven machine, which will do as I say, yes.' But he was smiling. 'It's going to be kept busy, full-time. It's going to revolutionise our life. It's the latest, the top model, and "Man enough for the job", according to its purveyors. User-friendly, they assure me; the State of the Art.'

Vanessa frowned at the stream of jargon, even though he used it satirically. 'User-friendly, is it?' She stepped closer, to peer at the controls. 'I bet it wouldn't be friendly to me if I tried using it. I'm—what does Mark call me?—computer illiterate.'

'Oh, you just have to show them who's boss,' Rick announced airily. Then, breaking into a wry grin, he admitted, 'As a matter of fact, I'm not really much of a micro-man myself. If it can help me with some real, creative work, I'll bother with it. Otherwise...' he was looking at her intently, serious now. 'That's where you come in.'

'Me?' She blinked. 'I've just told you, I'm useless. I've got a block about the whole...Carol's Ken was saying, only a few weeks ago, we ought to go computerised in *Doorsteps*, to take some of the admin burden off, but then he's crazy about them. Lives and breathes them. Carol told him...oh!' She broke off, as light began to dawn.

Rick was nodding, smiling as she spoke. He drained his drink and set the glass down on the desk. Confronting her, he thrust both thumbs into the belt of his jeans.

'I think you're catching my drift. I'll need a microchip wizard, to take charge of this wonderful creature. Someone who'll make sure it continues to be our servant and not our master, who knows their way around every convoluted corner of it. Someone who can translate the book-of-words standing on their head, who can always be on hand to programme and store and print, and generally be the middle man.'

'Someone like Ken?'

'Someone local,' he went on, 'a permanent post, with flexible hours to suit us and himself. I'll pay the right man top rates. He'll earn every penny, though, I'll see to that.'

'Oh, Rick!' Vanessa was touched and flabbergasted. The power of those magic wands: affluence, influence...

'Do you think Carol's Ken might be interested? Do you think he's as expert and reliable as you say? Would his employers corroborate that?'

'Ken's brilliant, and I'm sure they would. They had to put him on the hit list—last in, first out, you know—but they were genuinely sorry to do it. He loves your kind of music. It's just the sort of job he'd enjoy.' Vanessa was breathless, dark eyes shining. 'He's serious and dependable, but independent, too—he has a sort of flair—I've heard him say he'd rather work on his own, or in something less rigid...and Carol would be so...oh, Rick!'

In the confined space, she was reaching a hand towards him. The dregs slopped from her glass to the floor, but this time she never noticed. 'You're an angel!' she declared.

Rick rescued her empty glass and put it down next to his. Then, as her arms came up spontaneously to wind themselves about his neck, he caught her round the waist. Her radiant face was upturned, the naturally olive tone of her skin flushed a delicate rose in this harsh, fluorescent light.

'Lady, I'm no angel. I'm only too human.' There was humour in his blue gaze, steady on hers, although he did not smile. 'But I'm user-friendly,' he added, his hold tightening on her waist.

'The State of the Art.' Vanessa smiled, but the surge of elation was giving way to something deeper... slower... altogether richer.

'Mister Fixit, that's me.' His voice had dropped, low and husky. 'I knew I was going to need someone, ages ago, when I first planned this—but when you told me about Lacey being made redundant it seemed fortuitous...'

'It was meant.' Vanessa was glowing. 'When I tell Carol...!'

'No. Don't say a word to Carol, not till I've approached Ken.' It was a command, but a justified one, and she did not demur. 'If you agree to the idea, I'll take action—when I'm ready. Just leave me their phone number, and I'll contact him at home, very soon. OK?'

'Of course, you're right. It's just that I—I know how pleased and excited she'll be—and I do...'

'You do care about her. You do care, I know that, Vanessa. It's one of your qualities that makes me...'

Words were becoming unnecessary. His fingers were hard on her waist, then straying down over her hips in the cord jeans; then sliding up, over the soft sweatshirt, until they reached her breasts, and his thumbs were touching and exploring the curves and peaks. Then his hands were on her back, moulding, and her body swayed, instinctively in rhythm with those possessive movements.

Hardly knowing it, she was murmuring, 'Thank you, Rick. For all this, and—earlier this evening—and...'

Her face was searching for his, her body straining to his. Only one language seemed adequate to express this turmoil of feelings. Gratitude, and appreciation, and others, much more personal. But it was a language she had never been fluent in, and now had almost forgotten—or thought she had . . .

When his mouth feathered from her forehead to her temple, across her cheek, until at last it discovered hers, she was poised, yearning for that fusion. She returned the kiss with equal ardency and real eloquence, without inhibition. When she drew away, her lips were passionately parted, her eyes heavy, her hair loose about her face.

'I can see I'm going to have to please you more often!' The chuckle was no more than a rumble in his throat. 'I know they say virtue is its own reward, but I can't claim to be totally altruistic in all this, Vanessa . . .'

He leaned down to seek her out a second time, but she evaded him. 'First let me tell you *my* news. One good turn . . .'

Unwillingly he released her, just far enough to watch as he listened.

'Not news, exactly. More of a—shift of attitude.' It wasn't easy, now she was faced with it, finding the right words for this new, private concession between them, but Vanessa was determined to have everything clear. Honesty—clarity—parts of that language they were sharing, as important as the physical contact . . .

'Maybe I can guess.' Tenderly, with affectionate irony, he set about making it easier on her. 'Does it concern Mark, by any chance?'

She wasn't letting herself off that lightly. Before he could spell it out, she drew herself up straight and firm. 'I've decided he should come to you—to Totem—for the work experience after all. If you'll still have him,' she added, with a new humility.

'Vanessa, you're great!' He hugged her, his chin rough on her glossy hair. She knew from his tone that he was smiling.

'It's not because of tonight.' Her voice was muffled against his shoulder, but emphatic all the same. 'I made up my mind quite a while ago. I only came up to the church tonight so that I could tell you.'

Rick held her at arm's length again. 'Regretting it?'

'You know I'm not.'

'I'm glad to hear that. And I'm glad about Mark. It'll be a good thing for him, and for me, and perhaps even for you, Vanessa, who knows?'

'Who knows?' she echoed. With this man, she might believe anything.

'We'll sort it out when this current promotion's over. I'll have a lull then, and I'll need a break. There's no great rush, is there?'

'As long as it's well before his exams. The school breaks up for the Easter holidays next week. I thought we might try and fix it then?'

'Sounds fine. I'll get my electronic brain on to it. I think I can just about manage that much, before the true expert steps in...'

Rick's words faded as he crept close again, to claim another of those endless kisses, which must finally end if both parties were not to drown, or suffocate, or crumple to the floor.

Even when it ended, Rick's voice seemed a continuation of the caress—no more than a flutter of meaning, a breath in her ear. 'I don't know about you, but I feel—overlooked in here. There's something voyeuristic about all this hardware. Could I make us more comfortable next door?'

'I thought you'd never ask,' Vanessa murmured. Hand in hand, pressed close, never cutting the electric circuit, they made their way back to the lounge—and then, by unspoken consent, through to the bedroom. Rick switched off all the lights except a small bedside lamp, drew the curtains, kicked his shoes off and knelt to remove Vanessa's. Then he was pulling her down, on top of him, among crisp, plump folds of duvet.

A double duvet. A double bed. Before she gave up making sense of her thoughts, Vanessa registered that much. And why should it not be a double bed? Rick was single—fancy free. A man with more chances and offers, no doubt, than almost any other in the country; what else would she expect? Strangest of all, why didn't she care?

Just now all she cared about was his mouth on hers again. On hers, in hers—then colonising further, as his fingers freed buttons and zips, pushed aside clothes. Then his hands were blazing their trail, finding their unerring path across her skin, scorching wherever they touched. His lips and tongue followed, adding fuel, so that she flamed and gasped, clinging—pleading—but for less, or more?

When she was all but naked, he rolled her over beneath him, so that he could gaze down at her. Then he studied her, savouring every line, contour, summit and valley with his eyes, before charting them with his hands. Closing his eyes now, he revelled in her, relished the silken roundness of her;

and it seemed only natural and right—only part of opening herself up to him and all these new feelings—when he demanded access to her most secret places. Reverently delicate, igniting a subtle fire which spread through from the core of her to every fibre, so that she gasped again and cried his name aloud.

By intuition, rather than reason, she recognised her own elemental power over him, inextricable from this tormenting need for him. Her woman's need, to be invaded, to possess by being possessed. To be initiated into that deepest mystery, which is no mystery, but the simplest, most universal experience in the world.

Free of his shirt, he was smooth, firm, sinuous. Her hands, and all her senses, rejoiced in this new communication; the feel of his back, shoulders, chest—lean, yet surprisingly strong—his flat stomach. Then she was struggling with the buckle of his belt, and the fastenings of his jeans...the essence of him, his male self, was there, rising to her, and she wanted it. She wanted him, the whole man, just as he wanted her. Their fulfilment would be total, and mutual. Pent-up instincts writhed, suppressed and sublimated far too long. He was her destiny, her release. The passionate reality of her nature was awakened at last, a Sleeping Beauty. Rick Seymour, her full-blooded knight, her fairy-tale prince...

Her clumsy efforts to reach him heightened his desire, only too evidently. But his response was devastatingly unexpected.

He moved aside, off her. One strong hand gripped hers, prevented what she was doing. The other came up to smooth the tousled hair from her burning brow—stroke the fiery cheeks.

She stared up into his face, suspended, literally racked. He stared back, equally torn, yet controlled and extraordinarily calm. When at last he spoke, his voice was hoarse—intimate, but tough.

'Vanessa. I can't let you—I can't do this.'

'Rick?' She lay completely still. Already the acute tension was easing, that throbbing need dying down, cooled by his deliberate withdrawal. 'Why? It's—I'm . . .'

He gathered her into his arms. 'Listen to me, woman. I've got two—no, three—things to say to you. Will you listen, and try not to be hurt?'

'I'll listen.' She pulled back, to see into his face. I'll listen but I can't guarantee not to be hurt, she finished the sentence to herself.

'First a question. Are you on the pill, or anything?'

She shook her head. Confused, sheepish—and a great deal too late—she blushed to the roots. 'No. I don't—I've never . . .'

'Quite.' He nodded. 'I didn't think you had. When you do, Vanessa, it's going to be—well, it's not going to be like this. The man who enjoys that privilege will be honoured, but along with the greatest honours come the greatest responsibilities. No one knows that better than I do. And this is the greatest one I can think of. OK, so two lives and happinesses might be in the balance, here; but three would be one too many. You take my point?'

'Oh, yes, I take your point, Rick.' He was horribly, embarrassingly right. How could she, of all people, have been so thoughtless, so careless—so selfish, so unlike herself? How *could* she?

'Hey, don't look so agonised! There's nothing wrong with what's happened—or nearly happened.

There's everything right about it! It was wonderful, the way you gave—it was moving, Vanessa, and I...'

His voice softened, causing Vanessa to melt and tingle all over, all over again. 'That brings me to the second point. I wasn't joking the other day, when I talked to you about being chaste and chased. In my line of business, you either go under, or keep out. Drugs—drink—sex. The whole relentless spectacular. Me, I prefer to stay clear of all that, Vanessa. I decided that, the moment I climbed on the pop bandwagon—the moment I saw where it could take me.'

'Yes, I know,' she muttered.

'It's nothing but a load of empty ego-massaging.' He was angry now, bitter—not directed at her, of course, but alarming none the less. 'My fans can believe what they like. Their fantasies are their own problem, and the media don't help. It's all part of the show I voluntarily entered into, so I can't complain. But privately—in real life—I never play the field.'

'I didn't think you did, or I wouldn't have...'

It was only partly true, but he nodded understandingly as he interrupted. 'No, I'm sure you didn't, but I had to make all this clear, especially to you. Oh, don't get me wrong, I've had my flings over the years. I'm not a callow youth, and I'm not without feelings—appetites—weaknesses, or without experience.'

'No.' That much was all too obvious, even to Vanessa's green self.

'But I never committed myself—and I learned that, when you're as beset by temptation as I am, the best thing is not to commit yourself sexually without committing yourself emotionally. In my situation, integrity is even more crucial than in anyone else's. It's part of me—part of the code I live by. You see what I mean?'

'Of course. I'm not surprised, Rick. And I'm not—hurt.' She swallowed. Exposed, perhaps, but not hurt. 'I hadn't thought it all through. I just went with my feelings. I suppose that's another thing I have to thank you for.' Her colour was high, but her tone grew less shrill. 'Saving me from...'

'It *wouldn't* have been a fate worse than death! Or so I'd like to flatter myself.'

'I was about to say, saving me from myself,' she retorted with dignity.

'You may well thank me! Let me tell you, it was the most selfless act I ever did. Going on, letting it happen, would have been the most...the best...'

It was his turn to falter; hers to reach out and touch his cheek, offering reassurance and strength. 'No, Rick, you were right. I'm just raw and green and all wound up inside. I got carried away, much further than I ever meant to. The excitement of what happened in the church, then all the rest...'

All the rest summed up a multitude, a positive tidal wave of passions and emotions. She knew that, and so did he, but he let it pass, nodding sagely as he released her, so that they could both lean back more comfortably against the pillows.

'Thanks for being so mature and sympathetic. One day, it'll be made up to you, Vanessa, and that's a promise; by someone worthy of you.'

Who could be more worthy than him? 'Made up to you too, I hope?' She grinned at him now. 'Not much fun for a man, I've always understood. A bit painful, being encouraged, and then...'

'If anyone's been guilty of teasing tonight,' he said drily, 'I reckon it was me.'

The laughter was short, but shared. 'We'll survive.' Vanessa felt remarkably calm and confident now—able to be candid and outspoken as she never had before with any other person, despite the fact that she had very few clothes on; and despite the events of the last hour. 'What a pair!' she observed. 'This clean-living, high-principled, universal sex symbol—and this repressed, frustrated virgin! Strip off their veneer—and she's anybody's, and he's nobody's!'

'Don't be so hard on yourself, Vanessa. You weren't about to be just anybody's. You were about to be mine, and I'm not likely to forget that.' He paused, briefly. 'And I'm certainly not nobody's. Just not till I choose—till the moment's right...'

'OK, OK, you've made your point. That was your third point, I suppose?' For some reason, Vanessa felt anxious, the beginnings of an inner agitation. Tiredness, probably; the shock, physical and...

'Something like that; I sort of lost count. Now it's getting late, and I think we should make ourselves decent, and I should drive you home before Mark gets worried. Have you told him, by the way, about the work experience?'

'Oh yes, he was thrilled. He can't wait.' She was already off the bed and pulling on her jeans. Rick was right again, damn him.

'I'm looking forward to meeting him. Might be the start of a meteoric career, you never know.'

She restricted her scepticism to the merest grunt. This was a time of change and possibility, there was no denying that, even if some of the new pathways were not running quite straight and smooth. But when it came to the subject of Rick's kind of music—his *other* kind of music—Vanessa still reserved the right to her doubts.

Fifteen minutes later, in his car, Rick turned to face her. Mark had dutifully left the porch light on, but otherwise her street and house were in darkness.

'One last thing, before you flee to your unblemished bed.'

'Before *we* flee,' she corrected, 'to *our* unblemished beds. By the way, why do you have a double bed, if you're so...?'

'I never claimed to be pure as the driven snow. I only said...'

'Yes, yes. I'm sorry I asked, I don't really want to know.'

'Yes, you do, and I'm going to tell you. It's more civilised, that's why. I like space, I like to spread out. And I keep my options open. I establish my territory and make full use of it, so when the opportunity finally presents itself—the *right* opportunity—I'm...'

'Ready to leap at it, I see. Rick, I wasn't serious. I just...'

One arm round her shoulders, he pulled her close so that he could kiss her lightly on the forehead and cheek. 'Yes, you were. You *are* serious. I like serious people. I like serious women. Now I've got a serious proposition to put to you.'

'Oh yes?' She shifted round, peering through the gloom, trying to fathom his expression and tone.

'You know it's our Bristol gig on Saturday? The climax of this last tour, a big occasion for us. It's a sell-out, and there'll be full coverage—TV, radio, all that—and we're cutting a live album. I'd like you to be there, Vanessa.'

In an evening of challenges, this must be the culminating jolt. 'Me?'

'Yes, you. Why not? Is it so amazing?'

'But I...'

'I know, I know. You don't care for *that* kind of music. You don't grace it with the label of music. But you've surprised yourself tonight, Vanessa— twice. Why not try for the hat-trick?'

Somewhere inside, there was another of those rusty creaks, as if things were on the move. 'Would I be able to bring Mark?'

'Great idea.'

'I'll—I'll think about it. What should I do, if we decide...'

'I'll tell you what. Tomorrow I'll drop two—no, three—complimentary tickets in here. Best seats, front stalls, with automatic access to backstage afterwards. No pressure—no assumptions, Vanessa. I'd like you to be there, but if you can't bring yourself to... well, you can send Mark, with a couple of friends. And if you come, he can still bring a friend. How's that?'

'I—all right. Thanks.'

'If you do come, at least you'll have tried—and I shall be pleased, for several reasons. If you don't—well, I'll understand. And either way, I'll be seeing you. Up at the church, maybe?' he suggested, with studied nonchalance. 'When rehearsals get under way?'

'Maybe.' She neither confirmed nor denied the possibility. She needed time alone now, to pull all these strands together. She picked up her bag and jacket, opening the car door. 'Thanks for—for everything, Rick.'

'No, Vanessa. Thank *you*. Now, get some rest, it's been quite a night.'

He started the engine, watched her safely across the threshold, then pulled away from the kerb.

CHAPTER ELEVEN

'Whatever solid state you're in,
 Brother, you're gonna spin,
 Keep those feet on the ground,
 Feel it, it's going round . . .'

THIS was the kind of pop music which audiences listen to, every nerve stretched; not the kind where they scream mindless approval. Totem was the kind of band people respond to with heads and hearts— not on some frantic, childish high.

'Smooth that oil in, sister, mind that blister,
 Get your tan, have your fun,
 You can afford to forget
 The Dark Side of the Sun . . .'

Rick was always at the centre of the magic web, raising hell on his keyboards, clashing and stomping his percussion, or simply singing his own lyrics. He performed this—his other kind of music—with precisely the same virtuoso vigour. He adapted his mellow, subtle tone to the demands of broadcasting and the mass venue; but only just, as if making a generous concession to public expectation.

Yet every nuance and syllable came clearly through. Vanessa felt these words, tunes and harmonies—in her flesh, under her skin, in places where no other sounds had ever quite penetrated. It wasn't just because Rick stood there, up in the spotlight. As she shared his performance, Vanessa understood his message for the first time. His kind of music, more than any other kind, was food for the senses and the emotions; and hers were just uncurling into life after an enforced hibernation.

No wonder she was susceptible to it now, against her every personal taboo. All around her, every female in that auditorium sighed, knowing how effortlessly they could fall in love with Rick Seymour. If only, if only... But he was available to them in fantasies, and that had to be enough. Even the men responded with warm admiration, or envy—or, in Mark's and Stewart's cases, plain hero-worship. Society must have its potent symbols, its totems.

For Vanessa, the exhilaration was entirely private. She was busy swinging from total resistance to total immersion—the zeal of a convert. Overripe for enlightenment, now she was succumbing completely.

Rick himself was breathtaking in action. The whole scene was shattering. The power of the beat, the shifting myriad laser colours, the shared heat and regenerated energy of the audience. But as she gazed at Rick, he was no glorified god—nor some overblown stranger. He was himself, only more so. The essential man she had come to know so well, so fast. If she hadn't already, she fell in love with him at that moment.

As for Ellie, she was superb, gorgeously vivid as ever—perfect foil to the men in their unassuming jeans and shirts. They made no compromises to image or fashion, this group, presenting themselves straight. Their music and its messages were what mattered. But Ellie pranced and gyrated, living out every phrase, belting out the songs in that throaty velvet voice, sometimes adding an exotic touch of bongos, tambourine, maraccas. Soft or loud, solo or in duet with Rick, she shone.

Vanessa felt sick: with the excitement, the pride of actually knowing these people—and the shame of having dismissed their art so long and so lightly.

Now it was over—and the end of the last song. Vanessa was aware of acute disappointment, intermingled with relief. It was so intense, she really couldn't take much more—and yet she could have gone on all night! But the audience was clapping and screaming for another encore—and Mark and Stewart, beside her, were almost apoplectic with reflected glamour—and Rick was stepping forward to the microphone again, holding up a hand. An expectant silence swelled.

'This will be positively our final number tonight. It's a new song, you won't have heard it before. Wherever she is, I'd like to dedicate it to a friend of mine. Vanessa. Thank you.'

In the darkness of the auditorium, Vanessa went hot, then cold: crimson, then ashen. Mark and Stewart stared round at her, open-mouthed, then at one another. This was beyond their wildest dreams. Absolutely over the top! Back at school, they'd be basking in fame.

Mark's glance at his sister held another, new expression too. He was beginning to understand, just a little. Something had been happening here— something pretty miraculous—something that went a lot further and deeper than his work experience and all that. Amazing enough, the way Vanessa had brought him to this concert; now he suspected he owed more to Rick Seymour than he had begun to guess.

He turned back to watch the band as it struck up into a melodic intro, full of vibrant harmonies. This time Rick did not play any instrument but stood at the centre, relaxed, casual, addressing each listener individually. He couldn't see them individually, of course, against those fierce lights. But Vanessa knew he was singing to her, direct to her, whether she was actually in the hall or not.

'My beat ain't gonna eat you.
Let it warm you, let it heat you,
Let me moan, let me screech,
Only let me reach you.
I'm alive, I'm not Art, don't set me apart,
Hear me in your body, feel me in your heart.'

'I feel you, I hear you.' It was a low murmur, inaudible to anyone else, but her feelings were suffocating—bursting—straining to fly to where Rick stood, to home in where they belonged; at last undisciplined and unrepressed.

The next ten minutes were a blur. The shouting and applause; the surging forward, with the rest of the audience, then the jostle to that holy of holies—the artists' rooms, backstage. Mark and Stewart, like junior bodyguards, took over, flanking her, guiding her and generally protecting and organising her. They were fairly bowled over by the concert, but it was evident to them that Vanessa's mind was absolutely blown. She needed looking after, and they were the men to do it.

Most of the people obviously knew each other, calling, embracing, heady with success, enjoying the acclaim whether direct or indirect. The group, and their hangers-on: the privileged few—exhausted but elated, buzzing about, gabbling their congratulations.

Only Rick stood in the midst of the crush, serene apart from a certain glint in the depths of the blue eyes—as sharp and lucid as Vanessa had seen them. Nothing could spoil or tarnish the man. Her respect for him grew. What had she done, to deserve his interest in her? Was this the full extent of it, or...?

Their eyes met, and she held out both hands. Ignoring the others milling around him in that sweaty, noisy room, he strode over and took them. He was hot and hoarse, but utterly controlled.

'Vanessa, I knew you'd come. I knew you were here.'

'Of course I'm here.' Her voice was surprisingly steady. 'Rick, may I introduce Mark and his friend Stewart?'

'Mark, Stewart. It's great to meet you.' He dropped Vanessa's hands, in order to shake theirs. 'Did you enjoy it?'

Stewart was literally tongue-tied. Mark, more poised, nodded eagerly. 'Fantastic. Brilliant.'

'That's good.' Rick accepted the accolade with a gracious grin. 'Well, I gather we'll be seeing quite a lot of each other soon, eh? Between us, we've managed to persuade this stubborn sister of yours to let you risk corruption at Totem's hands?'

'It's very kind of you.' Mark's dark eyes were enquiring, as they turned from Rick to Vanessa. He was increasingly alerted to these undercurrents flowing between them.

'Not kind, Mark. I wanted to do it, very much—you ask your sister. I kicked up a big fuss when she wasn't going to let me.'

'Something like that.' Vanessa muttered agreement, smiling faintly, turning away—suddenly abashed.

Rick was looking quizzically at her. 'I expect you've hated every second of this evening, haven't you?'

'No.' She swung back to face him. 'I loved it, I really loved it. Thanks, Rick, for—you know—asking me here.'

The statement might not have been effusive, but her shining eyes and clear tone reinforced it. Reading the layers beneath it, Rick smiled. She might sound like a polite guest at a party, taking her leave, but she was telling him something far deeper. The nervous, narrow-minded years—the years when pain had led to prejudice and paralysis—were over.

'It's OK. I'm glad you enjoyed it.' The words were gruff, but softened by a new sweetness.

Then Ellie was bustling up, to be hugged and appreciated, and insisting on meeting the two boys, crooning over them until they were charmed almost beyond the limits of teenage endurance. And Vanessa was being presented to the rest of the band, soon mingling and chatting like old friends. Champagne corks popped, and everyone sparkled as effervescently as the contents of the bottles.

Rick was caught up in the throng, apparently forgetting all about her. Mission accomplished? Triumphant on all fronts, now he could afford to let the whole thing drop, having achieved its aim?

But then he was detaching himself from a tribe of squawking press interviewers, crossing the room to materialise at Vanessa's side.

'Come in here. I've got to talk to you.'

Quietly, discreetly, he drew her into a tiny dressing-room, hardly more than a closet. Closing the door, he leaned back against it, instantly blotting out the crowd and creating a cocoon around the two of them. In the warm darkness he pulled her to him, enfolding her. They stood, motionless, in their own oasis of peace, while the sounds of merriment went on—just a door's thickness away, yet it could have been a hundred miles.

Then he was drawing back, lifting her chin with one finger so that he could stare into her face. When he bent to kiss her, it was the gentlest, tenderest contact she had ever known.

'Did you really like the concert, Vanessa?'

'It was magnificent. Your music is wonderful. Your words are stunning. Your performance is fantastic. What can I say?'

'You seem to have said a fair bit.' She couldn't see him, but the smile filled his voice.

'Rick, I want to say thank you. For the song.'

'Don't mention it. As long as you picked up the message.'

'Loud and clear. But I haven't finished...I mean, I want to thank you for—for everything, not just that. I've been stupid, closed my mind... I was scared and blocked, but at least now I realise it, and I'll make sure it doesn't happen any more. I'm free, and it's down to you, and I want you to know I'm grateful.'

'Steady on.' He laid a finger on her lips. 'I don't expect such total capitulation in my women. I enjoy a fight, remember?'

'This isn't submission, only recognition. Anyway, I'm only just beginning. I don't suppose I'll find *all* rock music as easy to like as yours. You'll have to give me plenty of help with the rest of my education...'

Rick was chuckling, holding her close again. 'The first creaky opening of the mind, that's the real hurdle, the biggest step. There's nowhere to go from here but ahead.' He nuzzled the top of her hair. 'You're a brave, honest lady, with the strength of character to admit you might have been wrong. You're going to get all the help I can give you. You're going to be well and truly educated. Between us, Mark and I will see to that. Never mind *his* work experience—yours is about to get under way!'

'Rick, I...' In the dimness, her eyes were raised to his.

'What is it, Vanessa?' he whispered back, hands on her shoulders.

'I love you.' The words were as natural as breathing. But now she was waiting, suspended, conscious of a growing fear in the silence.

Rick gazed at her thoughtfully, tracing the outline of one soft cheek with a fingertip. The suspense swelled, unbearable.

'Are you sure it isn't just a touch of the old magic? You know, the charisma: the smell of the greasepaint, the roar of the crowds? Don't say anything you might regret in the morning.'

He was fending her off. A coldness lurked at the edge of this new flood of confidence: the hint of a panic. 'Don't say that! I felt this way, before tonight. I've been feeling this way since...'

But then she subsided. He was wrong, but he was right too. The emotions were real enough, but it had been tonight they had crashed through to the surface—under the influence of this heightened atmosphere.

She looked up at Rick. He was smiling; before she could interpret the smile, he was leaning down to kiss her again. It was very sweet, and very long. At last he broke away, and Vanessa's dazed mind only half registered the words he was murmuring, close to her ear.

'What the hell, anyway? Why does it matter, the reasons you love me—as long as you really do? I ought to have more faith in you, Vanessa Davies, of all people. If there's one woman in this wide world who isn't going to want me for my public image and nothing more—well, that one woman surely has to be you.'

'I loved you,' Vanessa stated, 'before I saw you on stage. Before I even thought I could ever *like* your kind of music.'

He pushed her away then, creating a distance between their bodies. She shivered at this deliberate cooling of the warm contact.

'You want the truth from me, Vanessa?'

There was a hardening in his tone. She nodded, but her stomach clenched as she stiffened herself, ready for the worst: rejection.

'The truth is, I was doomed, the moment you popped up in that church. This vision, conjured up by César Franck—this bolt from the blue—this divine gift. It was enough to turn a man religious.'

Apprehension was being edged out by incredulity. 'Doomed?'

'Doorsteps, I was a goner—a marked man, I tell you. I fell in love with you the moment your face appeared in that neat little rear-view mirror. I knew, the moment you spoke to me. Bang! A totally new experience. I still haven't recovered from the shock.'

A tide of joy surged. Her heart took in his meaning, long before her head dared take the risk. 'You fell...?'

'Why else do you think it's been such an obsession, wooing you over to my other kind of music? Why else do you suppose it's mattered so much to me, this whole business of Mark? Oh, I was angry at first, when you refused—when you stood in his way. But once I met you, got involved with you—well, it became personal.'

'It became pretty personal for me, too.' It was a wry response, but on a note of pure happiness.

'One thing I could see, straight away. I had a fight on my hands. Not just an intellectual one—a real, emotional one. If there was the smallest chance of a mature, stable, adult relationship, Vanessa, I had to penetrate this block of yours...push through to the real you.'

'Oh, Rick!' She had misconstrued him, all along the line. She had put his concern down to pride, or pique; the exaggerated urge to exorcise his own private ghosts, using Mark as a vehicle.

Now his involvement revealed itself as direct, focusing entirely on her. The realisation was awesome, and glorious—and laced with just a touch of shame.

'Thank you,' she said again. And this time, the actions that followed spoke decibels louder than the worn-out little phrase.

The silence in their enclosed space rose, extended, densely charged. Next door the sounds of revelry continued. Vanessa and Rick were oblivious, lost in each other.

But eventually their own names percolated through the private delight, piercing their mutual absorption.

'What's going on in there? Cut it out, you two!'

'This is a family show!'

'Put that girl down, Rick, you don't know where she's been!'

'Hey, man, aren't I always telling you, if it's groupies you want...'

'Rick? Vanessa?' A knock—Ellie's voice. 'Are you in here?'

'Come on.' Rick grinned, running a hand through his ruffled hair, then smoothing Vanessa's, away from her flushed brow. The instinctively possessive gesture caused her heart to lurch. 'We've got to brazen this thing out. We'll have to tell them, Vanessa.'

'Now? Just like that?'

'It's going to be fairly obvious,' he pointed out drily. 'Anyway, no time like the present. Mark's there—and the few people who really matter to me, too. I want them to know. Don't you?'

But Vanessa held back, uncertain. 'Know what, exactly?'

Catching her uncertain note, he took her hands again. 'That we're a pair. Partners, if you like. That from now on they can expect to see us, out and about together. My place, your place—around the place generally. Wherever life leads us. Does that make sense?'

'Oh, yes, it makes sense.' Put that way, it sounded perfect.

'It doesn't have to be anything—binding, Vanessa.' Rick was absolutely serious now, the blue eyes intense on hers. 'Nothing to alarm you, or pin